REWIND

Recent Titles by Vivien Armstrong from Severn House

CLOSE CALL
DEAD IN THE WATER
FOOL'S GOLD
FLY IN AMBER
THE WRONG ROAD

REWIND

Vivien Armstrong

This first world edition published in Great Britain 2001 by
SEVERN HOUSE PUBLISHERS LTD of
9–15 High Street, Sutton, Surrey SM1 1DF.
This first world edition published in the USA 2001 by
SEVERN HOUSE PUBLISHERS INC., of
595 Madison Avenue, New York, NY 10022.

British Library Cataloguing in Publication Data

Armstrong, Vivien
    Rewind
    1. Detective and mystery stories
    I. Title
    823.9'14 [F]

ISBN 0–7278–5699–5

Typeset by Palimpsest Book Production Limited,
Polmont, Stirlingshire, Scotland.
Printed and bound in Great Britain by
MPG Books Ltd, Bodmin, Cornwall.

One

H e picked up the bag of rubbish and dumped it in the shed. Holiday jobs were hard come by and two months as a pool attendant-cum-odd-jobber was only marginally more attractive than the only other work on offer that August: office boy at his father's plastics factory in Plymouth. And, apart from everything else, Plymouth was too far from Rosie.

The hotel job paid peanuts but was live-in and only an hour's drive from Rosie's place in Norwich. And Rose was a girl Simon Harris knew better than to leave unwooed till October released him from his stint with bloody Swan House.

The sky was ominously overcast, heavy seas breaking against the ruins of a wartime concrete pillbox which had long since tumbled on to the beach below as the crumbling coastline submitted to the appetite of the breakers. Simon reckoned the hotel itself would go crashing on to the beach before too many years passed. Good riddance.

The only remaining chore before breakfast was to tidy up the indoor pool, a small affair used mainly in the winter months and banned to children under twelve since the older guests complained of the kids' noisy appropriation of the jacuzzi. He slid back one of the patio doors and picked his way through the poolside chairs to unlock the boiler room. The pool area was rarely secured from the garden – in theory intruders were likely to be daunted by the two mile unmade-up road connecting the converted manor house to

1

the nearest village. Security was left up to the hotel guests themselves who, being mostly young couples and groups of friends, seemed unperturbed by the open house style of Swan House, delighted, in fact, that late night ravers from the Lowestoft discos were not faced with a locked front door after midnight. Out of season the rules tightened up, keys were turned and a night porter snoozed in the hallway.

The indoor pool had been added only two years before in a desperate effort to boost the winter bookings, "minibreaks" being the magic formula according to the trade journals. Tacked on to the old kitchens the pool annexe sported a jaunty Spanish style – pantiles and all. Plastic palms dotted the perimeter and wide patio doors offered a view of the sea. Under the glimmering early half-light the lumpy shapes of loungers lay abandoned like beach chairs on an empty film set. His footsteps echoed under the shell of the painted rafters, the fetid atmosphere freshened by the draught sifting through the open garden door. A towel and a bathrobe together with a single rubber flipflop lay strewn by the side of the hot tub, a whiff of chlorine sharpening the morning breeze.

He shoved back the chairs and, whistling to himself, fetched his sweepers and a bin from the utility room and switched on all the lights, picturing Rosie's tangled mop on the pillow, wishing himself snuggled up beside her at this ungodly hour, Simon never one to be up with the lark given the choice. Spotlights hit the water like laser beams, bouncing off the sparkling surface in rippling wavelets as he dipped his net into the deep end. Then he saw the body.

His heart skipped a beat and he leapt back, cannonballing into a tub of artificial palms. His pole split the dusty surface like a lance, refracting the image under the water into a thousand fragments.

She lay face down at the bottom of the pool, stark naked.

Lapped by the gentle flow from the inlets, long strands of her hair swirled as if to soundless rhythms, her limbs spread, starlike and white as bleached bone.

Stumbling into a clumsy trot, he made his way through the staff exit and along the brick passage to burst into the steamy hotel kitchen. Only the cook was already on duty. He looked up, scowling, but his irritation at the intrusion of one of the outside staff was instantly doused by Simon's ghastly pallor. Confused by his garbled words, Pascal shoved him ahead back down the unlit passageway, the two emerging from the darkness blinking, the piercingly azure water floodlit as if for a star performance.

The star herself, having slowly rotated in the flow, now lay belly-up like a dead fish, her small pointed breasts tiptilted, the dark bush below a rude contrast to the long bleached hair.

Greenfaced, Pascal bolted back to his kitchen and promptly vomited in the butler's sink, leaving Simon, now partly recovered, to make a tremulous 999 call. Only with the noisy arrival of two police cars surging to a halt on the gravel drive did Simon register that he had forgotten to inform the manageress. He listened to the crunch of boots approaching along the staff corridor, the hysterical volume of Mrs Mayo's objections to this unwarranted dawn raid growing ever louder, "malicious false alarm", "staff problems" etc. etc. percolating his numbed consciousness.

"Oh God, she's going to kill me for this," he moaned. Such unnecessary drama, such wanton disregard of the proprieties. He could hear it already. Well, he never thought this summer job much cop anyhow. But even a trainee pool attendant knows the unwritten rule about death in an hotel. Nobody dies under a hospitable roof. Never. Death is only admitted when the corpse is safely off the premises.

Poor fish of a girl, Simon thought. Whatever made you do it?

Two

G roups of hotel guests fluttered in the gardens like starlings, twittering excitedly as more police, eventually followed by an anonymous mortuary van, arrived and departed. Small children hopped about impatiently yanking at their parents' jeans, anxious to be down on the beach despite the lowering sky and the spatter of raindrops.

Mrs Mayo attempted to usher everyone into the dining room where coffee and croissants had been laid on as a damage limitation exercise until the inspector and his merry men gave the all clear. It really was too bad – just when the hotel bookings were looking up as well. She dashed from group to group mouthing earnest assurances that "All will be back to normal *very* soon. A tragic accident . . . a poor girl's foolishness, to swim alone at night . . ." It was indeed sad. Even the guests excited by the frisson of drama so unexpectedly spiking a dull summer break experienced a shiver of dismay. Such a pretty girl. Such a senseless waste of a young life.

Detective Inspector Ian Preston had commandeered the secretary's office, grilling the hapless receptionist who, trembling, produced the relevant paperwork. The police medic lingered on in the hallway, buttonholed by the wild-eyed manageress, attempting to stave off her questions with soothing phrases. Doctor Ramsay was anxious not to attract the wrath of the irascible young police inspector by disclosing any advance information. Preston had hauled him over the coals during that last case when

4

all he had been trying to do was to palliate the distress of the parents of an undergraduate who had thrown himself from the college tower. The death of one's child: the ultimate tragedy.

Preston laid into Tracey Lovelace with no such sensitivity. After all she wasn't related to the dead girl in the pool, was she? Barely set eyes on her in all probability.

"And you are quite certain she arrived alone this Adele Morrison?" he barked.

"Her car's still in the car park – you can see it from here. The blue MG."

He swivelled round to peer through the window. "Ah yes, very nice too."

Tracey sniffed into a ragged tissue, more than a little miffed that Mrs Mayo had left her to deal with all this while she fussed round the twitchy guests. To add to Tracey's misery the phone had never stopped ringing all morning; reporters from the Anglian Chronicle, not to mention several weekly local papers intent on muscling in on what was obviously a scoop with very little staying power. Even so, the drowning of a holidaymaker was always a circulation boost, especially in August when news of any sort was in short supply. The fact that the body was naked seemed to be the most interesting factor as far as the hacks were concerned. And goodness knows how they had found out that little titbit so quickly. From Simon, that stupid pool attendant, at a guess.

Ian Preston ran his finger down the names in the guest book, passing it over to his sergeant who was still working his way through a sheaf of booking forms.

"So we know nothing more about this Mrs Morrison other than her address in Cambridge? No credit card?"

"She wasn't paying."

"Her partner made the booking?"

"I've already told you all that."

"Mr Brendon Underwood, London SW11?"

"That's right."

"And he paid in cash? Isn't that rather unusual?"

"Not if you're married," Tracey snapped.

"Ah, right. But he booked this short stay only last Wednesday?"

"Not even a cheap Weekend Break," she retorted, rallying at last, fed up with the tone of this irritable flatfoot. What was he so narked about? Presumably Sunday was his day off. Tough. Or maybe drownings were two a penny in his line of work and he'd got a backlog of more important cases to deal with she conceded – always a girl to take a kindlier view of human nature than working in a run-down seaside hotel fostered.

Tracey would probably have taken a less charitable tack if the bloke was not, as it happened, a bit of a hunk under that ratty disposition. Better looking than most of the people round here at any rate. Tall. Black haired. A swarthy skin slightly pockmarked. And the bluest eyes she had seen off the cinema screen. But it was the odd socks which warmed her heart. Clearly a man living alone. No woman would send the poor devil off to work wearing one blue and one black sock, would she?

"Eh what?" she muttered.

"Describe this man who paid in cash," Ian Preston doggedly repeated. The sergeant looked up, grinning, as the Guvnor subjected the poor female to another flurry of questions about the presumably illicit rendezvous of Mr Brendon Underwood and the late Mrs Morrison.

Tracey fished in her bag and produced a pack of cigarettes. "D'you mind?" she said, snatching at a cigarette before he had a chance to object, her blue varnished nails flickering under the strip lighting as she struggled with her lighter. The inspector leaned back raising an eyebrow as his sergeant gallantly dropped his papers on to the floor to light a match for her.

6

"Thanks. Mrs Mayo don't let me smoke in here," she confided to the junior plod, "but I've never been this close to an accident like this before and it gives me . . ."

"And what makes you think it was an accident?" Preston cut in. "You *knew* this Adele Morrison?"

"No! But I seen her before."

"She's stayed here?"

"Three or four times since I started here."

"Which was?"

"Two and a half years ago. Nice lady she was, always full of fun, big tipper an' all – not like most of the people who fetch up here out of season."

"So she wasn't just a summer visitor?"

"No. Last time she come was just after Christmas, our quiet time."

"With Underwood?"

"No. With an American couple. Lovely people," she added, nervously fingering dangly earrings.

"Come off it, Tracey. What was Adele Morrison up to?"

The girl blushed, losing what temporary confidence she had scrabbled together since lighting up.

"Look, why bug me? Get Mrs Mayo in here. She knows as much as me or anybody else!"

Preston raised a hand in mute surrender, miming contrition.

"OK Tracey. Relax. Just tell me what you know and then you can get back to your knitting."

The sergeant smiled at her, nodding encouragement, and after a mulish shrug of her thin shoulders, Tracey spilled the beans.

"Right. Well . . . Adele was a real business lady, no sort of tart. Underwood was an exception, an older bloke, not a boyfriend type at all. Adele was freelance but mostly worked with estate agencies in Cambridge."

"Doing what?"

"She explained it all to Mrs Mayo one time. She was what she called a property finder."

"Does searches for clients looking to buy a house?"

"Yeah. But she was independent, wasn't hooked up with any property scam, on the take or nothin'. People from abroad or business people with only weekends to sift through the ads pay people like her to suss out the potential. She wasn't an estate agent, more of a time saver."

"Gets a search fee up front and a commission on any sale, sir," the sergeant put in. "It's a nice way of getting round the country and a smart operator can earn thousands a year with all expenses paid."

"And gets to meet rich people," Tracey agreed, the alluring prospect of a job like Adele Morrison's glimmering in her imagination like Halley's comet.

"And the American couple she brought here in January were clients?"

"Yeah. They was looking for a weekend place not too far from his work in Cambridge they said. He was some sort of scientist I think."

"And do you remember how long they stayed? And their name and address? Mrs Morrison didn't get any special rate for bringing people here, did she?"

"No. Never even asked. All these questions. Your sergeant can look it up in the bookings. The Americans had nothing to do with it. Why bother them?"

"I'm trying to fill in the picture, Tracey. We've no next-of-kin so far. No-one's answering her phone at home. Divorced perhaps? Underwood is not at home either and some information from her other clients or her associates in the property business might give us a lead. This Mr Underwood. It wasn't strictly business, was it?"

The girl stubbed out her cigarette, looking worried. "Well, yes and no. Mr Underwood was looking at houses and Adele borrowed some local maps from the office to plan some sort of itinerary – she'd left her maps in the

8

car and it was pissing down with rain. But there was more to it."

"You sensed a bit of romance lurking in there, Tracey?" he wheedled, the blue eyes now steely.

"Well, you don't have to be Sherlock Holmes to work that one out. Mr Underwood booked two double rooms but they only used number sixteen. Ask Doreen, she done the beds."

"The chambermaid?"

"One of 'em. Doreen Smalley. Gone off now but back at six."

"And was this booking made by phone?"

"No. He called in himself last week."

"Gave his credit card number?"

"No. Paid in advance. In fifties."

"Excellent memory you've got there, Tracey. Ever thought of joining the force?"

"I wouldn't like the company."

The sergeant coughed, glad to see how quickly the girl had perked up since the interrogation started.

She continued without pausing, looking the inspector straight in the eye.

"Adele recommended Swan House most particular he said but he wanted to see the leisure facilities himself if I wouldn't mind. I said we didn't have no gym or sauna or nothin' but he liked the beach and checked the chlorine content of the two swimming pools with Simon – said he was allergic to too much chemicals. Polite. No side to him at all. Lucky to get a cancellation as it happens, August being our busy time."

"Chatty, was he?"

"Yeah. Nice man, Mr Underwood. Lucky girl I thought to meself at the time, a lovely job like that showing people round all them nice houses, having a flash car and everythin'."

"And Mr Underwood. Did he have a flash car?"

"No idea."

"Don't guests log in their car registration numbers when they arrive?"

"Not specially. There's plenty of parking. It's a pretty free and easy place as far as the guests are concerned. Flexible mealtimes, no hassle about kids trailing sand and stuff up the stairs. Different rules for the rest of us though," she added, tightlipped.

"No complaints from the visitors then?"

"Well, now that you come to mention it, there was a bit of a do last night. The old girl in one of the single rooms overlooking the sea rung through on the night line and woke Mrs Mayo – she was telling me about it just as your lot bust in this morning and we thought . . ."

The inspector gathered up his papers and pushed back his chair, suddenly exhausted by all this hotel chit-chat. Ian Preston had recently transferred from Ipswich and already suspected this career move to be a mistake. The sergeant leapt up, aware of the dangerous boredom clouding the inspector's eye, Preston's acerbic manner with the ladies already a byword down at the station.

"Er, you were saying . . . Sergeant Fraser courteously interjected . . . "This elderly person. She complained to the manageress?"

"After one o'clock, Mrs Mayo said. 'Not what one would expect at Swan House, Tracey,'" she mimicked. "The people in the next room was having one hell of a barney according to Miss Moffatt. Carrying on something chronic, swearing and slamming doors. And it must have been loud to wake up Miss Moffatt because the old bag drinks like a fish – plonks herself in the bar till closing time – and out like a light once her head hits the pillow I'd say."

Preston was already at the door, stiff with irritation, frowning heavily at the sergeant who seemed to have all the time in the world for office totty.

"The manageress had to break it up?" asked Sergeant Fraser.

"No. While Miss Moffatt was still on the phone, it all went quiet and Mrs Mayo smoothed her down. Promised to speak severely to the couple in the next room first thing in the morning."

"So?"

"That's the terrible thing. The pair in the next room was Mr Underwood and Adele Morrison."

Three

Ian Preston went in search of the manageress, finally cornering her in the dining room where a gaggle of holidaymakers filled in their time with Mrs Mayo's free coffee break while glumly regarding the drizzle speckling the sea view. The atmosphere had darkened, the air of excitement earlier in the morning now dampened by the suspicion that bad luck was stalking Swan House.

Mrs Mayo sat slumped at her usual corner table, desultorily spooning the froth in her cappuccino, keeping Doctor Ramsay company while he waited for the inspector. They spoke in whispers, hushed by the air of expectation in which the hotel seemed poised.

Ian Preston quietly entered and pulled a chair over to their table, waving away the waitress with her coffee pot. He nodded in greeting and pitched straight into the woman in charge.

"Perhaps we could re-examine Mrs Morrison's room?" he said. "You have completed your enquiries for the moment I take it, Doctor?"

He agreed, sensing a dismissal, forewarned by the sergeant that his report would be taken apart word by word by this nitpicking D.I. Charlie Ramsay was their new police surgeon fresh from a stint with a team studying the bloodbaths of Accident and Emergency in Manchester. Drowning was a first since he arrived here. He would have to give the poor girl on the mortuary slab a thorough going-over before committing himself to paper. He finished his coffee at a gulp, passing a hand through his crop of ginger hair. He wore jeans and a tee shirt under a faded blazer, the Sunday morning call-out catching him just as he and Tilly were off to Southwold. Moving to East Anglia had been his wife's idea prompted by her asthma, and after only six months on the coast, he could rejoice in the roses in her cheeks, the ubiquitous "puffer" already receding from Tilly's anxious priorities.

Rising, he said, "I'll get back to you, Inspector," and picked up his bag, sketching a farewell towards the manageress who looked up, glassy eyed, still shell-shocked by the horrible turn of events.

She finished her coffee and excused herself to speak to the chef, returning promptly to usher her unwelcome interloper upstairs.

Swan House was still an attractive pile, Preston conceded. The building conversion had been limited to additional fire exits, two metal stairways linking the upper floors to the car park and striped awnings shading the dining room from the mid-day sun, currently conspicuously absent. The house was late Victorian, mullioned and oak panelled, the wide staircase creaking like a galleon as the two made their way to room sixteen.

Preston followed the woman closely, admiring her firm calves and neat behind, guessing Mrs Mayo to be a well-preserved forty-five or even fifty. No Mr Mayo on the scene it would seem: the lady bore the undeniable confidence of an owner/occupier. And where was the proprietor of Swan House?

They paused at a door at the end of the landing, a woman P.C. hovering outside. The inspector motioned her to follow them and the three entered Adele Morrison's room in single file, Mrs Mayo glancing round with professional indifference at the mess.

By contrast Ian Preston was irritated, assuming from his first brief visit earlier that the place had been taken apart by the sergeant and his sidekick who had been detailed to search for a suicide note – but they denied it. Nothing had been found.

The room was in chaos: drawers hanging open, clothing strewn on the chairs, make-up littering the bathroom. The bed had not been slept in and, neat as an unwrapped parcel, was in stark contrast to the surrounding disaster area. He gazed about, tightlipped. He'd seen all this before. Adele Morrison may have been a top-notch professional woman but, behind the crammed itinerary and fancy trappings she was just another untidy cow like his ex-wife – the memory of whose blithe indifference to order still had the power to set his teeth on edge. He turned to face the policewoman who, alert as an alley cat, watched him circle the room.

"And it was already like this, constable?"

"Oh, yes, sir. We disturbed everything as little as possible."

"Her handbag?"

She pointed to a lizard-skin pochette in the middle of the magazines littering the coffee table. A bunch of white heather tied with trailing pink ribbons lay like a bridesmaid's bouquet on the polished wooden surface, an incongruous tribute amid the chaos.

"From the hotel?" he asked Mrs Mayo, pointing to the papery blooms already browning at the edges. 'A Welcome to Swan House' stunt?"

"Of course not!" she snapped. "They were only here for a few days."

"But Mrs Morrison introduced several guests out of season, didn't she? A useful contact I would have thought. Brought a better class of tourist perhaps? Worth a gesture especially as she paid full whack, didn't ask for any special rate so I've been told."

The woman flushed. "We put a fruit bowl in each of the de luxe rooms. The flowers were nothing to do with me," she added defiantly.

14

"No florist's delivery for Mrs Morrison then?"

"She could have bought the heather herself you know. In town. Before she came."

Preston looked sceptical. "From what I've seen Adele Morrison didn't look the type who needed to buy her own flowers. Ironic when you come to think about it. White heather's meant to be for good luck, isn't it? And today's the thirteenth. Just goes to show – superstition's a load of rubbish if your number's up."

He caught the tail end of the policewoman's smirk as he spun round to address her. "No greetings card anywhere, Wheeler? In her bag?"

"We checked thoroughly. Nothing. But there's a brief-case," she added, indicating a black leather item on the floor by the bed. "Combination locked."

"Pity." Preston laid the briefcase on the bed, weighing his options. Until the doctor came up with his report and a relative of some sort could be located, jemmying a locked briefcase might present problems.

"I'll take it," he said at last. "And the handbag."

The manageress eyed the two of them with undisguised rancour, having the impression that a straightforward accident might, in the wrong hands, be blown up out of all proportion.

"I need to clear this room, Inspector. It's booked from tomorrow. New guests . . ." she said, her voice fading under his bleak response.

"What about Mr Underwood's room?"

"Unused. They shared. None of my business," she said flatly. "He was due to stay one more night."

"Left unpaid extras?"

"No, nothing like that. Fifty pounds and his key left in an envelope in my office overnight. The money amply covered everything including a generous tip for the staff."

"Perhaps they had a row?"

Mrs Mayo shrugged. "Perhaps they did. Bear in mind,

Inspector, that Mr Underwood was a successful business-
man. He must have had an urgent message calling him
away, preventing him from finishing his viewings with
Mrs Morrison which she mentioned were stacked up right
through the weekend."

"Come off it, Mrs Mayo. They had a fight in this
room well after midnight. The lady in the next room
complained."

The woman paled, visibly shaken by his aggressive tone.
"The walls in this house are very solid. Miss Moffatt
sometimes gets a little confused with noises in the car
park – people returning from the clubs up the coast can
be a little disturbing."

"I notice the window's wide open. It was a humid night
last night. Perhaps Miss Moffatt liked fresh air too. Sound
carries, Mrs Mayo. Miss Moffatt may not be as ga-ga as
you imply."

"I implied nothing of the sort!"

"Well, I shall have to interview her in any case. She may
have heard Mr Underwood's unscheduled departure from
the car park, can put a time on it maybe? Now, where were
we? Ah yes. May we check the bathroom, Mrs Mayo? See
if anything's missing?"

The bathroom was equally untidy, the shower door
ajar, a moist bathmat scrabbled into a corner beside the
lavatory. A Cartier watch and a gold bracelet together
with a packet of contraceptive pills lay on the shelf over
the basin.

"No bath towels," Mrs Mayo muttered. "People take
absolutely no notice of the rules about taking hotel towels
on to the beach."

Preston glanced out at the sea now blurred by summer
rain. "Hardly beach weather, Mrs Mayo. But presumably
the towel and robe left by the pool came from this room."

"We don't supply bathrobes, but Doreen always puts two
big towels in every double room even if it's been booked as

a single. But I can't believe Mr Underwood is the sort to appropriate hotel linen." She frowned, mentally calculating missing items, finally admitting that stolen towels were par for the course in the summer season.

Preston cast a final look round, drawing Mrs Mayo to the door and pushing the constable ahead into the corridor.

"Stay here, Wheeler, and don't let anyone in till I say so. The doctor's report will clarify matters and if Sergeant Fraser can't locate a next-of-kin by tonight I'll drive to Cambridge in the morning and check out her house. Keys in the handbag?"

"Yes, sir, including the room key. And a diary. Mrs Morrison had an appointment with Frobisher & Kent, the big estate agency people in Cambridge. Monday morning. Twelve fifteen,' she added just to put his hat on straight. That was the trouble with new brooms: either all matey trying to smarm their way in or, like this one, tight-arsed.

Mrs Mayo closed the door and hung a "Do Not Disturb" notice. Preston relieved her of the housekeeper's key and handed it to the policewoman, grinning for the first time – his face lighting up put the girl right off her stroke just as she was beginning to feel she had got the hang of this new bloke.

Mrs Mayo fell into step beside him, deep in thought, wondering how long it would be before Mrs Angmering, the owner of Swan House, put in an appearance. She hoped her initial assurances had put the creature off. With luck she would still be at church and by Monday morning the whole dismal affair would be cleared up. Even so, the indoor pool must be closed till the end of the week at least, some sentimental busybody had already laid a bunch of limp freesias at the garden entrance to the annexe, a mark of sympathy presumably. She hoped it wouldn't catch on. After all, swimming accidents in August were hardly unheard of, were they?

"I want to have another word with the pool attendant."

"I'll tell him to see you in the office, shall I?"

"No. I'll be in the annexe later. Send him down after lunch, would you please, Mrs Mayo? I want to speak to this Miss Moffatt first. Perhaps she could meet me in the bar as soon as possible. It would come better from you. Just an informal chat, please don't alarm the old lady. Now, tell me, which would be the most direct route from Mrs Morrison's room to the indoor pool?"

"The lift. Here." She pressed the call button. Nothing happened.

"Bugger. Oh, sorry, Inspector. But everything's going wrong at once. That lift was only serviced last month. I'll ask Billy to check it. Come with me, we can get to the annexe via the back stairs."

Freda Mayo led him through a door marked Private, her heels clacking down the narrow uncarpeted staff access to the laundry room and kitchens. The kitchen was now at full throttle, Pascal bawling orders, the fragrant waft of roast beef grabbing Preston's empty stomach like an iron fist. He paused to have a word with the chef, confirming he had already signed his statement, rechecking the exact time he and Simon Harris had discovered the girl at the bottom of the pool.

She led the way through the arched passageway linking the kitchens to the annexe, retracing the steps of the two unfortunates who had found the body. The staff access emerged into a glazed ante-room overlooking the pool which was still mercilessly toplit, the loungers slewed just as before, the towel and bathrobe tossed aside and left by the jacuzzi. Only the body was missing.

They regarded the scene, the steady plop-plop of water sifting through the outlets accentuating their silence. The place was oppressively hot, the windows streaming with condensation. Preston knelt down to test the temperature of the water then slowly circled the small pool, scouring the perimeter for God knew what. Clues, Freda Mayo sourly

18

conjectured, glancing at her watch, anxious to tidy herself up before facing the expectant faces in the dining room. Luckily there had been no cancellations for Sunday lunch, always a moneyspinner, locals as well as non-residents crowding in for Pascal's special menu. In fact there were seven extra bookings. Gawpers at best. Reporters on the scrounge most likely.

"Don't let me keep you, Mrs Mayo," Preston smoothly assured her. "Just send down the pool attendant about one thirty, would you please? Simon, wasn't it?"

"Simon Harris. An intelligent boy – a UEA student. I'm sure you'll find him very cooperative."

She stumped off, turning as she reached the door to the changing rooms.

"Life saving certificate too," she added with a bitter laugh.

Four

The barman discreetly pointed out Miss Moffatt sitting at a corner table overlooking the sea. The bar was already crowded, augmented by several non-residents booked in for Sunday lunch, their visitor status underlined by smarter turnouts, the residents sporting their yachty togs as a badge of superiority.

A log fire burned in the grate, a cheering gesture brightening the darkly panelled lounge on a wet Sunday.

Preston put on his most charming smile as he greeted the old lady and signalled to the waiter. Miss Moffatt was clearly well past retirement age but spry, her eyes alert as a terrier's. She wore a mauve blouse and denim skirt but no stockings, her scrawny legs brown as beech leaves, her sandalled feet set firmly on the jazzy carpet.

"May I introduce myself, Miss Moffatt? My name's Preston. Detective Inspector. May I offer you an aperitif? This sad event's had me on the go since eight. Thirsty work, eh?" He ordered a gin and tonic for the lady and a lager for himself, wolfing a handful of peanuts just to keep his growling stomach in check. The old girl was likely to be, he quickly decided, an excellent witness, her wits unclouded by the alleged boozing which Tracey had disdainfully pointed out.

"Just a few questions, Miss Moffatt. This unfortunate young lady, Adele Morrison – did you have much contact with her? She occupied the next room to yours, I understand."

20

"Indeed she did. With her gentleman friend. A Mr Underwood. A charming couple looking at houses for sale. I thought at first they were seeking a home for themselves but Mrs Mayo explained that the young woman was some sort of estate agent and that Mr Underwood a prospective buyer." She spoke in a precise tone seemingly unconcerned by the complicated relationship of the couple whose voices had broken her sleep the previous night. Preston repeated the manageress's comments regarding her complaints about the row in the next room.

"Ah yes. I was extremely upset at the time but, in retrospect, ringing down and disturbing Mrs Mayo at one in the morning was quite unnecessary. Old ladies can be awfully self-centred, Inspector, not used to the ups and downs of modern living," she said with a smile. "In any event, the racket stopped quite quickly. A lovers' tiff," she added as she took a sip of her g & t.

"Can you recall the time exactly, Miss Moffatt?"

"Absolutely! Ten past one. I sleep like the dead as a rule and nothing disturbs me. But this row must have broken out suddenly and was certainly loud. My room is almost at the end of the corridor and number sixteen occupies the corner of the building so fortunately no-one else was disturbed by the noise."

"Were they fighting, Miss Moffatt? Were you frightened by what you overheard?"

She bridled. "No, of course not. I'm not such a silly old woman, Inspector. I've travelled all over the world in my time and cycled through Pakistan when I retired. My girls chipped in to buy a custom-built bicycle for me as a leaving present. I'd always said I dreamed of setting off on an adventure like that and once they had produced this beautiful machine there was no excuse, was there? I do talks about it from time to time you know. Ladies' luncheon clubs and Women's Institute meetings. Try to persuade these older people to get off their backsides and explore a little while they've still got breath in their bodies."

"You were a teacher?"

"Headmistress. A girls' school on the South Coast. But I digress. You were enquiring about the argument in the next room last night."

"Dare I ask if you heard the gist of it, Miss Moffatt? It was a hot night. Their window was open."

She sipped her gin and caught the inspector in a candid gaze.

"What I'm going to say will only reinforce your prejudices about nosy old women, Inspector Preston, and I wouldn't blame you. But I must admit I could only hear general banging and raised voices at first. Then I was rather naughty. I opened my own window and deliberately eavesdropped." She grinned, unabashed by this admission.

"And?"

"Oh, it wasn't anything original. The girl's voice was shrill and easily overheard but Mr Underwood was more subdued – I really had to crane my neck out to catch it all. I didn't repeat all of this to Mrs Mayo, of course. The man had had an urgent business call it seemed. Insisted on cutting his visit short, cancelling their Sunday appointments. Viewings I imagine."

"Purely business then? Not really an emotional argument?"

"Not at first. But all the time drawers were banging, doors slamming and the girl's appeals became quite hysterical. The tone changed."

"You became alarmed? Feared violence?"

"No, not that. I just became angry, felt the man was being unreasonable insisting on departing in the middle of the night like that. But then it turned into a series of sexual recriminations."

"Ah!"

She nodded. "And money, of course. That's always a

problem when a relationship sours, isn't it? They had been on holiday together it seemed. To New York and Martha's Vineyard. He had spent a lot of money on her he said, and if they split up she had nothing to complain about. At that I phoned Mrs Mayo – I had heard more than enough, was ashamed of myself by then to be honest, felt like a voyeur."

"But that was it?"

"Yes. The noise ceased as suddenly as it had started and I presume he drove straight back to London. I heard his car start up shortly after. He used to park it at the bottom of the fire escape which led down from our shared balcony."

"And you're quite certain of the time?"

"Absolutely certain. I lay awake for more than an hour after Mr Underwood had left but heard nothing more apart from that silly call tune on her mobile phone. I'd heard it before – it got on my nerves but was certainly distinctive, like some sort of bugle call."

"She received a phone call after he left?"

"Yes. But whether she answered or not I couldn't say. It was relatively quiet by then, I'd closed my window of course. I must have dozed off. Perhaps Mr Underwood wanted to apologise, make things up."

"Perhaps he did. Another drink, Miss Moffatt?"

"Why not? Make it a double, Inspector."

He fetched her another gin from the bar, the room now practically empty, diners already tucking into their roast beef.

"I have to go. It's been nice talking to you, Miss Moffatt. I'll get back to you later. You're staying for a few more days I take it?"

She smiled and Ian Preston caught a vestige of the charm which must have made her an attractive young woman.

"Indulge an old lady, Inspector," she said. "Why are you wearing odd socks? Is it a new vogue?"

He bent down to whisper in her ear. "An emergency,

Miss Moffatt. A secret between us. My ex appeared out of the blue this weekend with her new partner, demanding custody of our cat, Kenzo."

"A tug of love dispute?"

"'Fraid so. It has been a continuing bone of contention since the divorce. As it happens Kenzo's a bit of an old fogey when it comes to his attitude to the married state. Voted with his feet and disappeared till they had gone. My wife thought it was a deliberate ploy on my part – she came back last evening and searched the house while I was playing tennis."

"You should have changed the locks."

"They broke in through my kitchen window."

"No cat?"

"No cat. To spite me – I have an unenviable reputation for order – Samantha took one of each of my pairs of socks. Knew exactly the sort of thing that would wind me up. My early call-out on this case left me no choice. Odd socks. They were probably laughing themselves sick all the way home, imagining my fury. Sunday morning and no shops open. As it happens I had to check in here before breakfast in my official capacity. I was hoping no-one would notice," he ruefully added.

She raised a warning finger. "Sounds to me as if your wife knew you all too well. A partner so set in his ways must have been hard to live with. I expect her new man is less demanding."

His smile faded. "Her new 'man' is a female, Miss Moffatt. Being left for another man is bad enough, being left for a woman is vastly humiliating."

Five

Preston snatched a pub lunch in the village and got back to Swan House just on half past one.

Simon was there already, sweeping up outside, tidying litter and the smattering of dead leaves which had blown against the patio doors. The doors had been locked after the discovery of the body, with the rubber flipflop jammed into the lift exit at pool level as an emergency disabling device to prevent nosy parkers exploring the scene of the tragedy. He unlocked one of the glass doors and drew Simon inside, re-introducing himself to the lad who still seemed anxious, put off his stride by all the comings and goings.

The air in the enclosed space was humid, a faint mist rising from the jacuzzi, the light filtering through the patio doors bouncing reflections off the surface of the water to flicker on the ceiling. Preston could imagine the place in normal circumstances echoing with children's laughter, kids splashing at the shallow end where tiled steps extended across the whole width of the pool. Difficult to drown accidentally he thought. Even a poor swimmer should be able to struggle to the side or even make it to the steps at the shallow end. It was a smallish pool, no more than ten metres wide, the place now subtly lit from a single strip light leading to the changing rooms adjacent to the lift.

"Just a quick run-through, Simon. Just to get the feel of the place. Take me over your usual routine, would you? Starting at lock-up time last night. I presume you handle close-down most days?"

"Billy, the odd job man fills in on my night off but I only get one weekend off in three so yes, it was me got the short straw Saturday night."

"Right. You show me the ropes and I'll only butt in if there's anything I haven't quite grasped."

Simon Harris was a good looking guy, twenty-something at a guess Preston reckoned and probably a hit with the girls, what with those rippling pecs flexing under the yellow tee shirt and long brown legs striding round the poolside. He showed Preston the boiler room but averted his gaze from his net still bobbing in the water. Well spoken, too, not the usual tongue-tied temporary worker these seaside hotels put up with for the summer season.

"About nine o'clock every night I politely chuck out any stragglers and close the garden doors. Not often anyone still larking about here that late – they're usually having dinner by then and the little kids who are the ones likely to cause trouble are not allowed in here. Sometimes there's the odd smoochers in the jacuzzi hoping to have it to themselves but generally it's empty by nine."

"Then you switch off the jacuzzi, check out the changing rooms and make sure everyone's out before you lock up."

"Actually, I don't lock up. Mrs Mayo said not to bother as we're short of keys and anyway there's nothing much to pinch. The lights and jacuzzi are switched off in the boiler room overnight so it wouldn't be much fun for kids to break in after hours and, even if they did, the pool is clearly visible from the dining room which is only divided from the annexe by a stretch of grass. But, last thing, I hang a notice on both entrances which says 'Pool Closed till 7 am' which seems to do the trick."

"But anyone getting in after two am for instance wouldn't find it difficult?"

"No. If they'd stayed here before they'd probably have sussed out that the notice was just for show. And if there was a full moon like last night there would be enough light for a quiet splash about on your own. Quite romantic if you like that sort of thing."

"But to your knowledge nobody tried it."

"Well, once last month a rowdy crowd did have a bit of a rave in the outdoor pool after the pubs closed but Billy got down there and soon cleared them out. Along this coast it's generally too cold for midnight swimming parties even if everyone's pissed and, believe me, any noise would soon cause ructions in the office. But, yeah, once or twice I guessed someone had been down for an early dip. You can always tell."

"So last night you locked up the boiler room as usual. Tidied the chairs for instance? No lost property or stuff left behind last night?"

"Definitely not. Not at nine." Simon frowned, determined to put his side of the story before Mrs Mayo or that bloody Billy who was always on his back about timekeeping put the boot in. "That towel and dressing gown thing were definitely not there when I closed up."

"The dead girl's?"

"Presumably. And I always empty the laundry basket outside the changing rooms before I go off duty so the place is pretty clear for the early morning lot and all I have to do first thing is switch on, do a quick clean-up and check the chlorine levels."

"Swimmers before breakfast?"

"Sure. Only a few but there's always someone who likes to get the pool to themselves first thing. Obviously there was no-one that early today or I wouldn't have been the sad bastard who got to find the body."

"Absolutely. Show me the changing rooms, Simon. Give me the whole night-time routine just to make sure I've got everything clear."

Simon led the way into the men's room, a small place sparsely set out with two rattan chairs, a plastic topped coffee table and a separate lavatory and hand basin. There was no shower cubicle. After a quick recce Preston followed Simon into the women's changing room which was basically similar apart from the addition of a long mirror and hair dryer. The dead girl had left no dry clothing for *après-swim* so presumably intended to nip back upstairs to change in her room after her naked solo.

"All pretty basic," Preston muttered, "but any guest who needed anything extra brought it down here with them. Body lotion and so on."

He flicked open the wicker laundry basket as they moved towards the lift. A single damp towel lay at the bottom which he pointed out to the boy who seemed nonplussed.

"Definitely not there last night," he insisted. "Must have belonged to the floater."

"But she didn't use this towel, did she? I asked my squad to bag up the towelling robe and stuff she left at the side of the pool and they would have taken the lot including the towel from her room."

"Maybe they dumped her hotel towel in the laundry basket. It is Swan House property you know, all the stuff's clearly marked and those red and blue towels stand out a mile on the beach. It's not evidence, is it? It wasn't bloody or anything?"

Preston ignored all this, sending Simon to fetch a freezer bag from the hotel kitchen and stowing the damp towel inside. They moved towards the lift door, still out of use. Preston bent down to extract the rubber flipflop, mate to the one packaged with Adele Morrison's bathrobe now awaiting collection by next-of-kin if ever they located anyone willing to claim the dead girl's personal effects.

"Stupid lot forgot this," he snapped.

"The lift's often jammed with a shoe or something, Inspector. Three times this week. I use the patio doors myself but guests don't realize they can always access the pool from the garden out of hours."

"Why stuff up the lift? Kids?"

Simon laughed. "Worse. Old biddies like Miss Moffatt. Caught her at it once or twice. So she can stop people getting down here early. She likes to have the pool to herself for a nice private swim. Does twenty lengths before breakfast at least twice a week she told me and, being a small pool, it's awkward if there's someone else getting in the way."

Preston grinned. "OK. Thanks Simon. I'm off back to the station for a bit of paperwork. You've signed your statement I gather. And Pascal too?"

"Sure. Not much to say really. My bad luck being first down here. Gave me one hell of a fright. I've never discovered a suicide before."

"You *knew* she was dead?"

"No doubt about it. Before I got on the UEA treadmill I did two years reading medicine at Cambridge. Failed. Got chucked out. My mum's never forgiven me. Always fancied having a doctor in the family."

"But you weren't tempted to fish her out? To try resuscitation?"

"No way. If I learned little else in that wasted two years, I could spot a stiff a mile off. I'd seen more than enough in the anatomy lab."

"What made you think it was suicide?"

Simon paused, suddenly wary. "Immediate reaction I suppose. Being naked struck me as odd for one thing. As if she was trying to score a point – make people sit up and take notice for once."

"A pretty girl like that? Hardly a typical victim in my book."

"How would you know?" he retorted, eyes sparking dangerously.

Preston struck out, a shot in the dark. "You knew her before, didn't you, Simon? When she'd stayed here with other business clients. Or did you get acquainted in

29

Cambridge? When you were a student with an eye for the girls? You being strictly on the level here, mate?"

Simon fell back, his face ashen. "Use your wits, Inspector. What would a woman like that want with a student?"

"But you *did* recognize her from before."

"Not at first. She was lying face down at the bottom of the pool. I'd spotted her at a distance on Friday, swanning round with that old boyfriend of hers but I kept out of range. Adele was trouble, a real little cockteaser. It was only when I came back with Pascal and the body had turned belly-up that I knew for sure. Look, it was no big thing, Inspector. I met her at Browns three years ago. I'd run out of cash – she bought me a drink and we got talking. We had a few laughs – nothing heavy. After that we used to meet if she was feeling foxy. She was starting to worry about her wrinkles, etcetera. I sort of cheered her up. In her line of business she never got the chance to meet anybody who wasn't out to screw her just as a one-night stand. Adele said she wanted to settle down which let me out long term. But even that old bloke she was shacking up with walked out on her."

"How do you know that?"

"I saw him check out. He was putting his case in the back of his BMW as I was coming back through the car park. I was surprised to see him and when he called me over I helped stow his golf bag and trolley in the boot. Said he had to go, urgent business, then he winked, all mates together type of thing. I assumed he had given Adele the elbow. Everybody seemed to eventually – she got quite a name for herself with the guys in my crowd, big-handed to start with but then got demanding, frightened blokes off. She could be very manipulative and my guess is he was married and getting pushed into a corner with her manoeuvring. Gave me a tenner, said he knew what it was like to have to work your way through college."

"Did she approach you at all this week?"

"No way! Listen, I was small fry. I doubt she even remembered me from three years ago and I keep my head down here. As far as I know she never saw me working in the gardens and, even if she did, she would be a fool to admit any quick-fix with a student to her caked-up old boy."

"You saw Mr Underwood drive off?"

"Yeah."

"And what time was this?"

"Half past one or thereabouts."

"And what were you doing lurking in the bushes in the small hours?"

"Just biked back from the village. Me and the bar staff at the Dog & Duck play poker after 'time'."

"I'll need another statement, Harris. I'll get back to you later."

He walked away, deep in thought, leaving the part-time pool attendant half afraid, half angry with himself at the way he had been caught up in the messy business. Fancy being tricked into admitting knowing Adele in Cambridge! Still, it might have come out anyway with a nitpicker like this bloody inspector on the sniff. What of it?

Preston took the lift to Reception, nodding curtly at Tracey on the desk as he strolled out into the afternoon drizzle.

The weather had not improved, a pale sun peeking between the clouds like a timorous swimmer at the water's edge. He sat in his car passing Adele Morrison's flipflop from hand to hand, contemplating the reaction of Simon Harris who at least admitted some sort of brief encounter with the dead girl. Why did the boy instinctively guess it was suicide?

Trouble was that Simon's remarks only fanned his own doubts about the accidental drowning scenario. When the towelling bathrobe had been examined and the women's changing room checked and rechecked it was all too obvious that Adele had no intention of going back to her room – she had not taken a key to let herself back in. She had wasted a lot of time both professionally and on a personal level with Underwood. It must have hit her hard.

Her client had checked out immediately after their row, had left his room key in the manageress's office together with a generous wad to cover his bar bills and tips and Simon Harris had seen him drive away. Morrison's own room key was not with her and the key to her room – room sixteen – had been located *inside* the locked bedroom. Adele Morrison was not planning to go back to her own room after her night swim. She wouldn't have been able to get in, would she?

But did she plan to knock up someone else? Simon even? Had the boy seen his chance to get a leg-over once the Big Spender was off the scene? Shot up to room sixteen via the fire escape and made her an offer which was bound to bolster her battered self-confidence. Underwood, by all accounts, was hardly a young stud. After a few nights between the sheets with an old fogey, Simon's suntanned attributes might have seemed very tempting.

Preston shrugged aside these spiralling conjectures and dragged his game plan back to basics.

Firstly, it was imperative to locate the girl's next-of-kin and secondly to find Brendon Underwood.

Six

A fter ten minutes sitting in the car contemplating his next move, Preston decided he had had more than enough of Swan House. The afternoon stretched ahead as grey as his mood; the doctor's report had yet to surface and Adele Morrison's business contacts would definitely be unavailable on a Sunday afternoon. With no next-of-kin to fill in the gaps and the only witness willing to admit any sort of relationship with the dead girl being a young pool attendant, his investigation was at a standstill.

Patience not being one of Preston's virtues, he was anxious to get this baffling case tied up. What had driven the stupid girl to slip down to the pool in the small hours? What sort of swimmer was she? And if she intended to top herself why was there no suicide note? On balance it must have been an accident. A frustrated female, too angry to sleep, literally making a splash after a row with a boyfriend who also happened to be her chief client. Tragic.

From the bar slips it was clear she and Underwood had dined in that Saturday night. And dined pretty well it would seem: champagne cocktails followed by two bottles of Chablis and a room service order for brandy to be sent up to number sixteen. Of course, it was unclear whether it was Adele or her generous host who was drinking the lion's share. But from his questioning of the bar staff, it would seem that the girl could certainly keep her end up in the alcohol stakes. In all probability they were both pretty tanked up that night – the half bottle of brandy delivered upstairs at eleven o'clock was almost depleted.

Even so, Simon Harris gave no indication that the Underwood chap was obviously over the limit when he saw him drive off at one thirty am. And as Underwood had intended to stay for the whole weekend a relaxed Saturday night in-house would substantiate Miss Moffatt's assertion that his recall to London was a genuine emergency. Unless, of course, as Simon suggested, the man had suddenly become disenchanted with the Morrison girl and decided to dump her before she really got a hold on him.

Until the pathologist's report specified the level of alcohol in the dead girl's blood any speculations about accidental drowning were just that. Preston's frustration at his lack of information exacerbated a temptation to call it a day and cool his heels until Monday morning. But it was not in his nature to throw in the towel so easily, the crucial question being the motive which led up to the dead girl's fatal swim.

One way to fill in the empty hours constructively would be to search her house. Bay Tree Cottage. He emptied her handbag on to the passenger seat: the usual stuff. Make-up bag, keys, two old biros, a dog-eared street map of Norwich, a wallet containing driving licence, credit cards and a wodge of tenners.

He stared at the photograph on the driving licence, the lively expression of the thirty-eight year old belying the apparent desperation Simon Harris had described. But maybe, to a student, any woman nearing forty was an old boiler however vibrantly attractive, in which case concentrating on needy older men would be a better bet. But even on the stretcher when the lads had fished her out of the pool Preston had to admit Adele Morrison was something of a stunner.

He shoved everything back in her bag and tossed it on the back seat with the briefcase and made a curt phone call to his sergeant. Fraser could mind the shop till he got back. He drove off without a backward glance at the ill-fated hotel perched on the edge of its crumbling clifftop.

It took longer to get to Cambridge than he anticipated, the disappointing weather driving holidaymakers to cut their weekend short. The route was also clogged by roadworks on the motorway and the summer bonus of caravans moving like tortoises, causing irrational bursts of impatience if no actual road rage.

Preston pulled over to look at the map. The woman's house sat well beyond the outskirts of the city, and turned out to be a farmworker's cottage prettied up with tubs of marigolds and a picket fence, the nearest neighbour's place a rundown mirror image half hidden behind an overgrown hedge. Talk about *Before & After* Preston mused, comparing the two brick cottages with his own recently purchased old forge still largely in its original state of semi-dereliction. House values being sky high within a twenty mile radius of Cambridge, he guessed Adele Morrison had paid a hefty price for her former labourer's cottage but being in the business, he guessed that even with her tasteful redecorations, she had calculated a nice little mark-up on any resale.

As a matter of courtesy he knocked and, after a decent interval, inserted her keys and let himself in. He found himself in a dark passageway, the latched doors leading off it all shut. A bathroom had been built on at the back and the kitchen doubled as a diner. Everywhere smelt pleasantly of beeswax and the downstairs rooms were, to his surprise, tidy and well dusted. Having assumed from the mayhem in room sixteen that Adele Morrison was just another slob, the neat but comfortably lived-in ambience gave him pause for thought. Perhaps there was a lover who was yet to surface.

He checked the two bedrooms, one leading off from the other, the second no more than a dressing room with a sofabed shoved against the wall, the place heated by off-peak storage heaters. The windows were tiny and Preston had to bend almost double to peer down into the minuscule garden laid out below. He experimentally opened drawers and cupboards, recognising designer labels from his sharing days with Samantha. Shoes were stacked on racks, all polished, winter boots standing to attention at the back.

It was something of a facer. Preston shrugged. No-one gets it right all the time he admitted with a grimace, wishing now he had paid more attention to her hotel room.

He clumped down the narrow stairway and sat at the kitchen table eyeing the open shelves with interest. The woman obviously lived alone, the absence of any macho clutter eliminating any phantom partner. Clearly she had not been much of a cook, the larder being sparsely stocked and the fridge containing nothing but a bottle of champagne, two organic yoghurts, a half-empty bottle of vodka and some Belgian chocolates. Presumably this bachelor girl ate out a lot and spent most of her time on the road viewing properties.

He wandered into the living room and poked about in her desk which yielded nothing more interesting than her bank statements and credit card accounts, all in enviable good nick. There were no shelves of books and only two framed photographs, one of an elderly man seated in a wheelchair and the other an enlarged snapshot of a continental pavement café, possibly French, featuring two women enjoying a glass of wine and laughing towards the camera. Neither of the two was recognisably Adele Morrison.

Preston stood in the centre of the room which was now darkening, the rainclouds shadowing what little sunshine struggled to percolate the small cottage windows. Despite the dimness, the place had an air of cheerfulness, most likely contributed by Adele's choice of bright rugs and a squashy sofa upholstered in terracotta linen.

He tried the answerphone. Only three messages: one from an optician's receptionist reminding Mrs Morrison that her spectacles were still awaiting collection, the second from a fellow called Backhouse requesting more information about a house in Aldeburgh. The third was from an estate agent calling himself Gary passing on a message from one of Adele's private clients, a man named Lawrence who urgently needed to contact her about a "final offer". Gary apologetically admitted giving the man her mobile number if that was all right? "The bloke sounded somewhat frantic, sweetie. Hope it wasn't one of your problem customers? Give me a buzz when you get back."

Preston removed the cassette and searched the drawers of a small side table under the window. This produced only a bundle of recent copies of *Country Life* heavily laced with post-it stickers bearing cryptic references to clients plus a theatre programme relating to a London performance of a play called "Ramola" in the summer of 1999, presumably a memento of a romantic evening. An accountant's letter about tax confirmed that Adele Morrison was not hamstrung by mortgage commitments. Lucky lady.

He replaced the magazines but retained the programme, feeling unaccountably confused. The dead woman remained a mystery: a complicated character both passionate and uninhibited and yet clearly businesslike. He shook his head and went outside to the car to fetch her handbag in order to try out some of the other keys. As he closed the car door someone shouted at him through the overgrown privet.

"Oi! What you after?"

A bent figure emerged from the parted foliage, a skinny Father Time look-alike only wanting a scythe.

Preston approached the boundary, flashing his ID. The

old geezer grabbed his arm, peering closely at the warrant card, giving the photo close scrutiny.

"Right then," he said. "What's your game? Poor girl drowned, didn't she? No crime in that. We heard about it on local radio. My Annie's all shook up, poor old gel, terrible shock it was. Always kept well away from water meself, could tell you a tale or two about getting in too deep."

"And you are?"

"Fred Adkins. Not that it's any business of you lot. Me and the missus've got the place next door. Belongs to the estate mind, but we still pays rent. Retired see. When me and Annie drops off the twig, the squire'll sell up our little cottage quick as winking. Like he done with old Mary's," he said, pointing at its twin that Adele Morrison had gussied up so smartly.

"Did you know Mrs Morrison?"

"My old woman used to clean the place for her – Adele moved in a couple of years ago. Can't tell what's what after this though. You know who'll take over next?"

"Sorry. No idea. Did Mrs Morrison have no family visiting? Friends?" he ventured.

"Divorced like all the youngsters these days. Some bloke did turn up the once though. My Annie was polishing round next door and this ponce wearing one of them striped scarves barges in shouting for Adele."

"A student?"

The old man laughed. "Nah! Turns out twas 'er 'ubby. Never seen *him* before. Professor Morrison. Says to Annie, 'I had arranged with my wife to collect the silver if you would be so good as to pack it up for me.' All lah-de-dah. My Annie calls me over and he shows us this university library card with his photo on it. Genuine enough. Still, I binned him out all the same. Annie weren't in the business of handing over the spoons to a stranger, were she? Said he'd call back when Adele was at home."

"Quite right too. What did he look like this ex-husband?"

"Oh a real toff and no mistake. Older than her by many a year. University teacher or sommat. Ten a penny in town," he spat. "You know the type: big talker, cheap old banger, scruffy tweed coat all over leather patches – could pick up a better 'n at the bloody charity shop."

"Did this Professor Morrison leave a telephone number? Any message for his wife?"

"Nah. But I clocked his 'ticulars from the library card. St Francis – that old college down past Kings. Bet he'll be back in a flash to grab her silver now the poor girl's dead."

"I'll check him out, shall I, Mr Adkins? Did Mrs Morrison have a new man, do you know?"

"No visitors. None at all. Place too small for entertaining the sort of folk she mixed with if you ask me. She weren't here much at all. Travelled a lot for her job, see."

"Right. Between you and me, Mr Adkins, and strictly off the record, did your wife like working for the lady?"

"No problem there. Left Annie's wages in the coffee pot if she was off on one of her trips. Regular payer, no complaint there."

"Kept the cottage tidy, did she?" Preston couldn't resist asking.

"Not too bad. Silly girl about locking up though. Often left the place wide open. I told her often enough. 'Adele,' I says, 'living in the country ain't what it was, my duck. Plenty of yobs roaming the lanes at night after the pubs close.' Just asking for trouble she was. Lucky she didn't get the place turned over, specially with her video and all that computer stuff she was into."

"Well, thanks again, Mr Adkins. You've been very helpful. Here's my card. Give me a ring, won't you, if you or your wife think of anything else which may help the Coroner?"

Preston sketched a farewell salute as he backed away,

scuttling into Adele's cottage like a ferret with the scent of blood.

Professor eh? And another oldie? Obviously keen on the more mature specimens this girl, and not necessarily just the rich ones either. He would have to look up this ex-husband of hers and insist on his co-operation prior to the inquest since no-one else had come forward.

Preston took a fresh look round the living room, suddenly aware that no "computer stuff" as described by the old man was apparent. Not so much as a laptop. Surely a person working from home would rely on computer records, especially in her line of business, working with several clients at once and no office back-up?

He placed the contents of her handbag on the coffee table and re-examined the driving licence. Date of birth? February 22nd. Harking back to Samantha's unimaginative choice of pin numbers, Preston had a brainwave and grabbed the locked briefcase. Two-two-two. And, hey presto, the combination lock unscrambled. Easy peasy!

The briefcase was stuffed with maps and estate agents' bumph, spare tights, a manicure set, sunglasses, an idiot-proof camera and a spare set of car keys. No diary except the freebie from Frobisher & Kent from her handbag in which she had tucked their letter confirming an appointment the following day. The diary seemed of little use apart from birthdays, shopping reminders and the odd telephone number. Clearly the woman relied on something else to keep her business appointments in line. There was no filofax. And no laptop.

He phoned Sergeant Fraser at Swan House and asked him to recheck her car and the empty room Underwood was supposed to occupy and make sure no laptop computer had been overlooked. He made himself a cup of coffee while he waited for Fraser to ring back, listlessly regarding his odd socks. Fraser got back to him within twenty minutes. No joy there. Certainly, some sort of engagements diary was missing and as he mulled over the problem another thought struck home – Miss Moffatt's assertion that Adele received a call on her mobile phone after Underwood had walked out on her. Where the devil was it?

He re-sorted the contents of the briefcase and checked the list of personal items Fraser confirmed had been put aside in room sixteen. No mobile phone. Could one of the hotel staff have pinched it? Hardly likely. In any case the WPC had been on duty outside the room from the moment the death had been reported.

The bloody thing couldn't just disappear, could it?

Seven

He glanced at his watch. Only six-thirty. Still time to flush out the ex-husband, Adele's professor. Trouble was the chance of any university man being in college during the long summer holiday was about as likely as swallows in December. But nothing ventured as they say.

Finding St Francis College was easy, getting inside rather more difficult. The main gates were locked, the porter's lodge incommunicado. He persisted with the bell and, after an infuriating delay, a stout party emerged from the main building and came dangerously within Preston's sights. Preston flashed his ID, issuing staccato demands of the porter who, being a man used to self-important personages shouting orders, remained unmoved.

"The college is closed, sir."

"I know that. But it's not a sinking ship, is it, man? I want to speak to Professor Morrison or whoever's in charge so make it quick. And while you're doing that I'll wait inside out of the rain if it's not too inconvenient. And what's your name, just for the record?"

"Brinton, sir," he said, buttoning his jacket as he reluctantly admitted the inspector, anticipating more ructions about the Bursar's rowdy retirement party last weekend. Funny the police asking for old Morrison by name though. The old fart never so much as got a parking ticket. They must have known Morrison was the only don who stuck to the college like a limpet even in August, the only senior man likely to be available.

"You're in luck, sir. Professor Morrison's working in his rooms, never much of a one for gadding about," the porter confided, now subtly loquacious, hoping to prise more details of this unexpected police enquiry. It wasn't about that bloody retirement party at all, he'd put his shirt on it. So what had the silly old bugger been up to to bring a detective inspector knocking him up on a Sunday night? Time would tell. Everything came out in the end and the porter's lodge was the first port of call for any scandal. Brinton phoned through from the lodge and mumbled into the internal line.

Preston was led across the quadrangle and through a maze of passages eventually to emerge via a narrow staircase on to a top floor landing where a middle-aged man stood waiting.

The professor peered myopically at his visitor as if he had awoken from a deep slumber. Preston curtly dismissed the porter and introduced himself.

"Ah yes. Oh, do come in. The college is closed, of course. As the only senior member in situ," he said with a nervous laugh, "I'm not sure if I can help you, Inspector, but do come in. Please."

He closed the door and led Preston to a seat by the fireplace, the small room dominated by an oversized desk and too many chairs, the atmosphere thick with cigarette smoke. The room gave no inkling of summer, the mullioned windows grimy and secured, the place full of heaps of clothing and empty take-away cartons like the temporary abode of a man on the run.

"You're off on holiday, Professor?"

"Not exactly. A short visit to an elderly aunt in Ireland. Just two days."

"Very nice too."

"And your business with the college?"

"Regretfully, my business is with you, Professor Morrison. A personal matter regarding your ex-wife."

"Oh yes."

Preston nodded, concluding the man's abstraction to be more of a congenital vagueness than incuriosity. Surely a normal reaction would have been, "Has there been an accident?" What else would bring a senior police officer to one's door on a Sunday night? Preston ploughed on, all too familiar with the unpalatable business of bringing bad news.

"Adele Morrison was found dead this morning. Drowned. It would seem there is no next-of-kin. Would you be willing to make a formal identification of the lady, Professor?"

Morrison visibly diminished before his eyes, the spare frame seemingly shrinking inside the tweed jacket, his eyes unfocussed. He removed his spectacles and took a deep breath, rubbing at the thick lenses with his handkerchief while staring at the window now rosy with the setting sun.

"I am very sorry to bring you this news, Professor. A terrible shock, of course. Such a young woman . . . We have been trying to find a relative and, as an ex-spouse, you may feel reluctant to help us."

Morrison replaced his glasses and glowered at the stranger who had invaded his private rooms, suddenly angry.

"Adele was my wife, sir! We were temporarily separated – no legal moves were made on either side to expunge our marriage vows let me assure you of that."

Preston drew back. "I had the impression a divorce . . ."

"Certainly not. Now, shall we continue?"

Preston hurried through the procedure, exacting an undertaking from the professor that he would present himself at the mortuary at ten o'clock the next day.

"And you will inform any other members of the family?"

"There is no family. Her father is dead. Her step-mother has lived in Canada for many years and Adele and she were never close. There is a sister, a half-sister to be exact, also living in Montreal so I believe. An actress," he added with asperity as if such a calling was on a par with a magdalene's. "I will telephone the lady – I have her address here somewhere, a Madame Schurrer she calls herself now."

"The step-mother?"

"Yes, of course. The sister is younger than Adele, the fruit of my late father-in-law's second marriage. Sylvie Reynolds."

Preston heaved himself out of the low armchair, anxious to be gone, feeling a wave of disgust sweep over him for no decent reason. But suddenly, it seemed inappropriate that the poor girl they had fished out of a hotel swimming pool had chained herself to this unattractive character, a man steeped in arrogance and as unlikely a partner in marriage as the Pope himself.

He returned to his car and made notes on the back of a typewritten report, telephoning Fraser to let him off the hook.

"I've found her husband, Fraser! In Cambridge."

"Blimey! You got a crystal ball, sir?"

"More luck than detection I'll admit. You can buzz off home now. Make sure the hotel rooms are secured and leave a constable on duty outside on the landing. We don't want any sightseers. The widower arrives in the morning, he's going to the morgue at ten to identify the body. Log it with the lab, will you? And make sure the doctor's report's on my desk first thing."

"What's this bloke's name?"

"The husband? Professor Morrison. I don't have anything else – didn't like to make it too officious seeing as I had to break the bad news. Actually, it's a weird set-up. I'll fill you in with the details later. Oh, and Fraser. You sure the girl's mobile's not knocking about? Kicked under the bed? Bundled up among all that tat strewn about number sixteen?"

"Absolutely."

"Not in the car?"

"I even checked the pockets of her bathrobe, sir, and went over the ladies' changing room with a toothcomb."

Preston sighed. Fraser was getting stroppy. It had been a long day. "Before you push off home try and catch the chambermaid. Doris something or other. Beaming that nice smile of yours, ask her if, on the quiet, she ever lets guests into their rooms when they've locked themselves out? With her pass key? Goes on all the time but they never like to admit it. And while you're about it, drop a heavy hint that we're looking for a mobile phone and a laptop computer."

"No bedder's going to admit knowing anything about guests' missing property!"

"Not directly, of course she's not. But if you give her a bit of a nudge, she might come up with something interesting. Ask her about Underwood. Just shake the tree a bit, Fraser. She should be on her rounds about now, turning down the beds while they're having dinner, lucky sods."

Fraser sounded unenthusiastic.

"It's a minor detail, I know, but we want to be away from bloody Swan House pronto, Fraser. The place's got bad vibes. Don't bother to ring me back tonight. See you in the morning. Nine o'clock sharp in my office. We'll square off the rough bits and sift through the pathology report so we can draft a report before the professor arrives."

"You anticipating snags, guv?"

"Absolutely not. I'm simply trying to accumulate as much information about this silly girl as I can. We don't even know if she could swim, do we? We'll ask the grieving husband."

"I thought she was divorced."

"Apparently not. Funny relationship if you ask me. But the prof's very touchy about any suggestion of divorce. Probably Catholic."

Preston confirmed some last-minute details with his sergeant before signing off, feeling much more cheerful after ten minutes' conversation with his oh-so-sensible sidekick.

He made a beeline for the nearest petrol station hoping to pick up a bacon sarni and a tin of cat food if not a new pair of socks. He grimaced at the thought of starting the week still hogtied by Samantha's little jape. He put through another call to Fraser.

"Just one more thing, Ted. Could you lend me a pair of socks in the morning?"

Eight

Ian Preston was back at his desk by eight poring over the police surgeon's initial report and cross referencing the jottings in his notebook.

Doctor Ramsay estimated that "The girl might have been dead for as much as four hours when the pool attendant raised the alarm but the temperature of the water precluded more exact calculations."

That put it, Preston guessed, no earlier than two or three in the morning.

"There was no evidence of foul play apart from minor bruising on the nape of the neck which might have been caused by energetic sexual play or a minor altercation."

Had the argument Miss Moffatt overheard involved force, actual bruising? The report went on to quote blood analysis figures regarding alcohol content and to query the chloride concentration in the blood.

Recent sexual activity was in evidence but not rape. Further forensic tests were suggested. "In view of the bruising and other outstanding questions I recommend a pathologist's investigation, thus confirming that the victim was not dead before she entered the water. Suicide cannot, of course, be ruled out. The Coroner's Officer has been informed and a formal request for a post mortem has been registered."

"Shit!"

Preston picked up his phone and got straight on to Doctor Ramsay at home.

"What's all this about a post mortem, Charlie? Bit strong, isn't it? On the evidence of a couple of love bites?"

"Bruises, Inspector, not bites."

"Same difference. Morrison was on a have-it-away-weekend. Stands to reason foreplay would get enthusiastic."

"I can only go on experience, Inspector, and, as a precaution, I suggest we take a careful look at all the circumstances. The alcohol level was dangerously high."

The doctor's tone was defensive, Preston's banter ignored. His response was supremely cautious from a police angle. Suspicious circumstances? What bloody suspicious circumstances?

He sighed. "OK. On your head be it. I'll attend the post mortem. Let me know when you've fixed it. Any reason why the husband can't make an ID while the poor kid's still in one piece?"

"Of course not. I'll see you at the mortuary later. We can discuss the details then. I know I'm new on this job, Inspector, but cutting corners is not my style. We'll put the death certificate on hold, shall we?"

Preston curtly broke off the discussion and lit a cigarette. The bloke was right, of course. But, bloody hell, what sort of a game would the pathologist think we're playing out here in the sticks? An hysterical female gets tanked up, has a fight with her boyfriend, then takes it upon herself to indulge in a midnight splash to cool off. Gets cramp or something, is out of her depth, loses her bearings in the dark, panics and drowns. All over in minutes. No suicide note, no witness and no evidence of anyone else involved. The only beneficiary was a clapped out university teacher who couldn't organise an infants' doggy paddle competition let alone murder by drowning. And that presupposed that the bug-eyed professor even knew to locate his wife at a seaside hotel in the middle of the night.

The time-scale was clear. Underwood was well off the scene before the girl even dipped her toe in the water. The pool attendant, Simon, might have been lurking about and spotted her skinny-dipping, of course, not to mention any sleepwalking pervert on the prowl.

Preston laughed, recognizing this propensity for flights of fancy as a serious professional impediment.

Luckily, Fraser turned up at that point bearing two styrofoam beakers of black coffee and a couple of dough-nuts. Preston greeted the sergeant with a grin, sending the doctor's report skittering across the desk and almost upsetting the coffee.

"Ramsay's hedging his bets. Wants a post mortem."

"Blimey! What's the husband going to say about that?"

Preston shrugged. "Ramsay's call. No skin off my nose but let's pray our sainted police surgeon isn't going to make a habit of it. The summer's not over yet: drownings up and down the coast all season'll soon clog up the pathology lab."

"What d'you think really happened?"

Preston leaned back in his chair, clasping his hands behind his head. "My impression is this woman Morrison was a bit of a gold digger on the quiet. Got it badly wrong with our learned professor who didn't strike me as having much in his back pocket but who knows? Adele Morrison was a quick learner and not up to her neck in debt by a long chalk. The cottage was unmortgaged" – he knew that much from her bank statements – "her job well paid and her wardrobe full of designer gear. Financially, she was on a roll and well able to go it alone. But maybe she felt the old biological clock ticking and Underwood let her down all round. Maybe she knew her luck had run out and was getting desperate. The pool attendant knew her before, you know."

"Simon Harris?"

"Yeah. Caught him on his back foot and he admitted

knowing her when he was a medical student at Cambridge years ago."

"Knew her? How well?"

"Bit of a frolic. Nothing heavy. But I'd like to shake him down a bit more. It's rumoured he wasn't the only bit of light entertainment Adele orchestrated even before she separated from Morrison."

"Do you want me to speak to him this morning while you're over at the mortuary? He might open up to someone more his own age."

"Hey! Watch it. Incidentally, did you bring those socks I asked for?"

Fraser produced a neat package, asking no questions.

"Ah, good man. I'll buy you another pair as soon as I can get to the shops."

A clerk popped her head round the door to warn them that the professor had already arrived. Preston jumped up, pressing the medical report into his sergeant's hand and swiftly changing his socks.

"I'll have to drive over to Cambridge again this morning, Fraser. Chase up her contacts, the estate agent mob, see what they've got to say about clients she was doing business with. Especially Underwood. I've tried his number three times already and no joy at all."

"The address he quoted on the hotel booking form was a company address, guv. An office phone number – nobody's likely to be in before ten, not in his line of work."

"Which is?"

"Antique books and maps. Underwood was some sort of dealer. First editions, old manuscripts and stuff."

"Wouldn't have thought there was much money in that."

Fraser shrugged. "Might have been a sideline."

"A front? Dealing in stolen museum library pieces? You heard anything, Fraser?"

"Not yet. But I'm making a few phone calls."

"Perhaps he didn't get rich from this book dealing lark. Could have won the lottery," he added with a smirk, tightening his tie and bolting from the office, leaving his "gofer" with the suspicion that perhaps his new boss had merely got off to a bad start with the other lads. Perhaps Preston's moodiness was only a "putting-your-hat-on-straight" device to establish his standing with the new team.

Preston ushered the professor into an interview room, a brightly furnished ante-room to the mortuary where the smell of fresh paintwork failed to disguise the unavoidable reek of chemicals seeping under the doors and along the corridors.

"Please take a seat, Professor Morrison. May I offer my condolences?"

The man nodded, glancing around the faux jollity of the waiting room with repugnance, choosing a straight-backed chair at the table. Preston seated himself opposite, opening a file and eyeing the bereaved with curiosity. He had, in fact, made an effort, substituting the tweed sports coat and flannels for a formal suit, the effect modified by his crumpled shirt, the points of the stiff collar having stabbed minute holes in the fabric.

"The attendant will call us when he's ready," Preston assured him, trying to dispel the irrational dislike made on that first impression in the college rooms. "May I complete my report? Your wife's full name?"

"Adele Priscilla Morrison. I have a copy of our marriage certificate here," he said, extracting a well-thumbed document from his breast pocket.

"Terrific! Saves time eh?" Preston responded with awful gusto, hearing his own hearty phrases plummet into the frigid atmosphere.

The details surprised him.

"You were married for eighteen years I see."

"My wife was too young if that's what you are implying. To save any impertinent questions, yes, she was, as you may have guessed, one of my students. An appalling scandal at the time but soon rectified. My career hardly suffered at all, Inspector, although certain buffoons still cannot forgive such unprofessional behaviour."

"They don't let you forget it, eh? Despite your subsequent separation? Despite your return to the fold?"

The professor stiffened. "Adele found university life stifling. I allowed her to take up employment to ease the ennui but it was not a success."

"The difference in your ages?"

"No, I meant her attempt at teaching was not a success."

"A teacher?" Preston failed to hide his astonishment.

Morrison ignored this, lighting a cigarette without a glance at his questioner, staring fixedly at a picture of a basket of kittens hanging over the mantelshelf.

"Adele never graduated, that was the trouble. The teaching post I procured for her at a private school did nothing to erase her boredom."

"You are head of the modern languages department I believe."

"Adele's French was passable, good enough for Finings House School but standards were low." He laughed, a hoarse cackle honed by years of nicotine abuse. "I used to tease her about it. *'Elle parle le francais comme une vache l'espagnol,'* I used to say. A garbled version originally phrased *'comme un Basque l'espagnol'* of course."

"Naturally. Now tell me, Professor Morrison. When did your wife move out?"

"Oh, I forget," he replied airily, waving aside this unpleasantry. "Surely none of this is relevant, Inspector."

"You must excuse me. But at this point I have no idea what I need to know and what not. I must warn you there are complications. The police surgeon has recommended a post mortem."

He sprang up, his lips trembling.

"On what authority?" he demanded.

"On medical grounds. We need to answer certain questions. Mrs Morrison could have hit her head diving in. No need to worry, I assure you."

"I thought you assured me it was an unfortunate accident. Simple drowning. An indoor pool – an unwise plunge in the dark . . ." he stuttered.

"Unquestionably true, Professor. But the pathologist needs to reassure the Coroner on all points. For example, could your wife actually swim?"

Morrison grew petulant, grinding out his cigarette in the tin ashtray, refusing to resume his seat. "Of course she could. Not well, I grant you, but certainly well enough for that piddling little hotel pool."

"You've seen it?"

Morrison spun round. "I know it well. Adele and I stayed at Swan House on our honeymoon. I myself return at regular intervals, always off season when the place is quiet – a sentimental journey you understand. The food's not bad either," he added crisply.

Preston frowned, fearing the whole case was slowly unravelling before his eyes.

The door opened and a lab technician nodded at the policeman, leading the two men into a stark Valhalla. Preston stood shoulder to shoulder with the professor as the sheet was raised, feeling a tremor pass through their proximity like an electric shock. The man suddenly turned, striding along the corridor like a soul possessed. Preston ran after him, catching his elbow and forcing him to stop. Morrison's eyes raged with emotion.

"There are some forms to sign, sir," Preston quietly insisted. "I am sorry to inflict this paperwork on you but the formalities you understand . . ."

"Yes, of course. I apologise."

"Here, let's sit in here for a moment. May I fetch you some tea? The shock . . ." He steered the shambling figure back into the interview room and produced papers from his briefcase. Morrison signed away his wife's decease with a firm signature, sternly pulling himself together.

"Poor Adele," he said, his eyes cold as death.

Nine

Driving to Cambridge twice in twenty-four hours was far from routine but the city had an enduring appeal to Preston despite the horrific traffic jams. He parked on a meter and made his way to Frobisher & Kent's agency.

The weather had brightened, the sun slanting through the medieval pinnacles like a sly madame intent on disproving her fickle reputation. He loosened his tie and picked his way through the streams of foreign students wobbling uncertainly on hired bicycles, screaming with fear and delight at the sheer absurdity of negotiating the ancient lanes and alleyways on two wheels.

The estate agent's main office was tastefully underwhelming, the windows displaying a mere handful of photographs of manor houses and the interiors of grand apartments in the city centre.

He crossed his fingers and asked for "Gary", keeping his police ID under wraps, not wishing to frighten the horses.

"Gary's lunching with a client at the Garden House. Shall I remind him you're here, Mr Preston? You had an appointment?"

The girl looked anxious, Gary's propensity for forgetting appointments probably legendary.

"No appointment but a matter of real urgency, I'm afraid. My business concerns Mrs Morrison's private clients – we wouldn't like to leave her people in the lurch, would we?"

The girl on the desk looked crestfallen, her eyes, Preston would swear, actually misting over.

"No, of course. Poor Adele. We've hardly had time to take it in. She was always popping in and out . . . How absolutely ghastly."

"Absolutely. Would you be awfully kind and ring Gary for me? I could wait here but it would probably be more private if I joined him for coffee when he's free. I won't keep him long."

The girl blew her nose and made mousy noises into the telephone, interrupting Gary's dessert, at a guess.

"In about half an hour?" she asked, amber eyes peering over her half-moon glasses causing Preston's attention to lurch. He longed to whisper that contact lenses would be even more alluring and wondered if his raw reactions to females in general were healing at last. Samantha's abrupt *volte face* had dealt a body blow which he had considered to be emotionally mortal. Maybe that scheming attempt of hers to steal his cat, not to mention the childish rape of his sock drawer had had a curative effect. He bounced his attention back to the dewy-eyed receptionist and nodded energetically, stepping out into the hot sunshine with a spring in his step. He decided to walk and made his way towards the river.

The exercise brought him out in a glow as they say, August now finally pulling out all the right climatic stops, giving the rain-washed pavements a positive sparkle.

Gary claimed him as he entered the coffee lounge, described by the receptionist right down to his brown suede loafers no doubt.

The estate agent held out his hand. "Gary Trenchard."

Preston identified himself, palming his police ID card into the outstretched hand, which was swiftly returned as if it was too hot to handle.

Gary looked every inch a young man on the rise, his blond forelock flopping over an untroubled brow, the cut of his lightweight suit quietly affluent. He signalled to order fresh coffee, moving his chair to sit closer to

Preston's at their corner table, anxious, no doubt, to keep their conversation discreet.

"How did you get on to me, Inspector?"

"Pure guesswork, Mr Trenchard. You left a message on Mrs Morrison's answerphone. If I had drawn a blank at Frobisher's I would have had to trail around the rest of the agencies looking for a 'Gary'."

"Ah, but I must assure you that Adele and I had only a very loose business relationship. She was not attached to my firm – we merely passed on any clients who needed help and, in return, she steered people towards appropriate properties."

"Appropriate properties on your books?"

"Not exclusively, Inspector. Adele Morrison spread her net wide."

"In her private life too?"

Gary flushed. "I wouldn't know. I'm gay myself."

Preston relaxed. "As we're being so candid, would you mind if I ran a few ideas past you? You have heard the gist of the fatal drowning at Swan House I take it?"

"It was graphically reported in the Anglian press."

"Then you do realize that Mrs Morrison's visit was not entirely business. Her client was a Mr Brendon Underwood."

"Underwood? Sorry, doesn't ring a bell. Adele's clients often contacted her through personal recommendation. She even talked about getting a website but whether it came to anything I've never bothered to find out."

"No information about Underwood then? Not even gossip in the staff room?"

"She never discussed her private life with me. Knew I wasn't interested."

Preston sighed, admitting defeat. He sipped his coffee, glancing around the elegant room with interest. There were few lingering summer visitors and, in view of the unfashionable time of year to be still in town, scarcely any obvious university types. Nevertheless, the place had a calm ambience, lacking the last-chance-saloon atmosphere of Swan House. Apart from the problem of the crumbling clifftop on which it perched and which would most certainly claim it within ten years, Swan House's air of desperation giddyingly disguised for the season was redolent of gas invisibly seeping from underground.

Why had Adele Morrison persisted in promoting the place to her clients? Surely her husband's mawkish affection for their honeymoon hotel would have the opposite effect on the woman she had become?

Preston changed tack. "Indulge my curiosity, Mr Trenchard. How much do you think a girl like Adele Morrison would make as a property consultant?"

Gary puffed out his cheeks. "Hard to say. At least seventy-five k. a year, probably more. As a lone operator she could run five, maybe eight clients at any one time. A non-refundable fee up front of say five hundred and a further one and a half percent of the purchase price as commission. She could also recommend builders and architects if required and probably got a kickback from them too."

"Why haven't you taken it up yourself? Sounds interesting."

Gary laughed. "Adele had to make it seem like fun, take the strain out of it for people too busy to handle the hassle on their own. She took time sifting out the 'dogs'. Clients like hers are impatient, don't want to waste time on useless viewings. Sometimes overseas firms offset these additional expenses for their important employees and settling in a foreign family quickly keeps everyone happy. People like Adele can smooth out any problems as part of the service, act as a sort of agony aunt to the wives whose VIP husbands are too busy to listen. Adele was brilliant at it. Took trouble finding out what the client was really looking for and, if necessary, steering them into avenues they'hadn't considered. It's a gift," he added, running a hand through his hair. "I prefer to stick to traditional methods myself."

"She had a thing going with her latest client. Was that unique?"

"No idea. Most of her clients were couples anyway. She specialised in second homes and country houses. We don't get many single men on our books either."

"Who said he was single? Maybe she was just sweetening the pill."

Gary looked uncomfortable and Preston decided he had overstepped the mark. "Look, I'm sorry to seem prurient but I need to dig up some sort of psychological profile for my report."

"It wasn't suicide, was it?"

"In my own view everything points to accidental death but the tests are still coming in and I've got a blank sheet here, Mr Trenchard. You sure Adele didn't confide in you? Anything you say is strictly confidential. You won't have to give evidence at the inquest. Nothing like that."

From a distance the deep conversation of the two men bunched together at the corner table must have appeared all too earnest for a warm summer afternoon but in the swiftly emptying coffee lounge amid the discreet laying of teatables it went unnoticed.

"OK. To be honest Adele could be a little sharp. Made a turn on every deal, ratchetted up the competition between agents and set us against each other, which is poison in this business."

"She got a bad name?"

"Not exactly. But we watched our backs. Giving that client of hers her mobile number was naughty of me. She hated anyone on her tail."

"Lawrence?"

"Can't remember his name now but I anticipated a bollocking from Adele next time we met. I felt I owed her one in the eye. She rubbished one of my properties to a guy I thought I had on board. Switched him on to something on Haverings' list before he'd even had a surveyor's report."

"Haverings in the city?"

"Sure. Can't miss it. Look, Inspector Preston, I've got to go. I've got an inspection booked at half-past. Here, take my card and pass it around the other agents. Just mention my name – they'll fill you in if there's anything to show up."

"Who took her photographs?"

"No-one. She relied on the agents' handouts. Glossy brochures which cost an arm and a leg to set up. We're talking about properties up to the million pound bracket. Adele shopped around, wasn't sniffy about the odd holiday home on the coast if it had potential but it wasn't worth wasting her time on the dross as she called it."

"Where did she get her experience?"

"Lost on me though she did once say she'd lived in Avignon for a while and she was a terrific linguist – fluent French and enough Spanish – I heard her yapping away at one of our clients at Easter. Adele's forte was a smooth line in patter and a nice bum. The suspicion was she worked in the European time-share market for a few years and later liaised with a French outfit offloading run-down chateaux. Just a little brainwave of mine from odd remarks she let drop occasionally – she never gave much away even when she was drunk and she could certainly shift the champers. Ironic she drowned. Funny way for a drinker to snuff it."

"But why return to Cambridge?"

"It's her home town, Inspector. Everyone needs roots and, with all the scientific work going on round here, Cambridge is something of a boom town."

They rose and shook hands, Preston glad at least to be wearing matching socks in such ritzy surroundings. They parted in the forecourt, Gary striding off to reclaim his Range Rover. Upwards of a hundred thou. a year he'd reckoned the Morrison woman earned. He whistled. Obviously he was in the wrong game.

When he got back to the station there was a note on his desk from Fraser.

"I got the girl who works in the agency below Under- wood's office to take a message. He's in Germany apparently – chasing up some sort of bible she said. As soon as he rings in she'll get him to call us. I didn't mention Morrison's name or any details about the case but hinted it was urgent."

Ten

Next day Preston was pulled off the Morrison enquiry to investigate the latest in a series of burglaries in Somerleyton. The Home Office pathologist made short work of the post mortem, coming down firmly on the side of accidental drowning.

At the inquest Preston gave an account of his own investigation and Underwood's statement settled the matter in the Coroner's mind. In the absence of any forensic evidence supporting any suspicion of foul play, together with the lack of any suicide note there wasn't much to argue about. Preston was satisfied and the owner of Swan House breathed a sigh of relief, no criticism of the hotel's safety standards coming up in court and no suggestion of suicide upheld to cast a pall on its reputation as a jolly seaside venue for family holidays.

The initial interview with Underwood had been dealt with by Fraser and his appearance later in court was Preston's first brief encounter with him. He proved a solid witness, a man of substance with no embarrassment about admitting the affair with his property consultant.

Underwood was closely examined on the nature of their final disagreement and calmly explained that Adele Morrison had placed more importance on their personal relationship than he.

"A lover's tiff?"

Underwood demurred. "I am a widower. I have no

63

intention of marrying again. Mrs Morrison had a different agenda."

"All too common with the ladies," the Coroner dryly remarked. Preston had the impression that the Coroner was keen to close the inquest before further titillating details drew the unwelcome attentions of the press to this unsavoury case.

Underwood's demeanour was serious but unapologetic. He wore a dark suit, the greyness of his hair accentuated by a near white beard neatly barbered. He answered every question frankly, leaving the court immediately afterwards, speaking to no-one. The dead woman's husband followed him out, staring at the receding vehicle with a look of bitter hatred. Perhaps the public disclosures about his wife's lifestyle had been more painful to Morrison than the loss itself, his innate desire for privacy shattered yet again by the woman who had rejected him to the end. He went back inside to await the Coroner's decision.

Professor Morrison was not called upon to give evidence as, to his obvious chagrin, it was revealed that the victim had left her husband several years before and was belatedly in the process of negotiating a divorce. This interesting piece of history was lobbed into the proceedings by the late Mrs Morrison's solicitor, an energetic lawyer from Cambridge called Fiona Blakestock. The professor slipped out after the close of play and drove away in his ramshackle Toyota before Preston had a chance to speak to him.

He did catch up with Fiona Blakestock, however, and found himself impulsively inviting her to lunch. The Old Fire Station restaurant stood conveniently near the court-house and offered a modest set lunch in rooms tricked out with chintz and teashop furniture.

"This is all very unexpected, Inspector," she said, settling herself in the chair he held out for her. The place was comfortably full on this airless afternoon but the majority of the customers preferred to sit in the garden where lunch tables had been set under the trees.

"It was good of you to take the trouble to attend, Ms Blakestock. Your character reference for the late Mrs Morrison was invaluable to the Coroner."

"I thought it important to stress Adele's strength of mind. She was not a quitter, Inspector, and . . ."

"Oh, call me Ian. Please. This is not an official occasion, Ms Blakestock. I'm new here, I enjoy meeting fellow professionals informally."

"Ah, well then, Ian, that's awfully nice to hear." Fiona Blakestock dimpled prettily, her dark good looks enhanced by the crisp white shirt and formal linen suit.

"A glass of wine?"

"Just one, I'm driving."

Preston ordered the drinks, a cold beer for himself and a chilled Chablis for his companion. She slipped off her jacket and glanced at the menu.

"You were saying before I rudely interrupted, Adele Morrison wasn't a quitter."

"Indeed not. I was determined to scotch any idea that her disappointment over that ghastly man Underwood might cause her to kill herself."

"You were friends?"

"Oh yes. We'd known each other since college. Before she messed up her life with the professor."

His pulse quickened. "You knew them both?"

"Adele and I shared a room initially. We hit it off straight away. There was a certain fragility about her in those days and I was considered the sensible one of the two."

"You surprise me. I was given the impression Adele was something of a hard cookie in business terms."

"She was a professional in a cut-throat game, Ian. The property market is high profile and she worked alone, handling several important contracts at any one time. But when we first met she was a babe in arms I assure you.

Her father was suffering from motor neurone disease, a desperately harrowing illness which is hell to witness. When Mr Reynolds insisted she left home to go away to university he knew his days were numbered. Her stepmother had departed to Canada the year before, taking her little sister with her. She had to cope with all this misery on her own and when the poor man mercifully passed away, she experienced a sort of breakdown. It was only when she returned to college and I thought she was beginning to cope that that bloody man got his hooks into her."

"The professor."

She nodded, her pale features fierce with emotion.

"She had inherited quite a lot of money too. Her stepmother had remarried in Canada and was entirely out of the picture so Mr Reynolds' estate was equally divided between the two girls, presumably in trust for Sylvie who was only twelve at the time."

"You think he seduced your friend for her money?"

"God, no! Even I don't say that. No, Larry Morrison was dazzled by Adele's vulnerability and she turned to him like a lifeline. He was her teacher. Students often get the hots for their lecturers and the odd one takes advantage. Morrison wasn't that type. He had no reputation for flirting with his students although, believe it or not, in those days he was charismatic if you like the academic type."

"You were a student of his too?"

"No way. But she once dragged me along to one of his lectures – some romantic guff about Baudelaire – and I could see she was smitten. He almost got away with the scandal but, after a bit of a showdown with the Dean, they got married and left Cambridge for a few years. Moved to Sussex and he pushed her into a teaching job at a stuffy boarding school. Just asking for trouble shoving her out on her own like that. She told me Larry said working for a living would do her a power of good but up till then she'd been at home every night at least."

"But the marriage was a success?"

Fiona shrugged. "No, the romance soon wore off and she got involved with a married man, another teacher at the school. Teaching was never Adele's scene and I bet she was glad when she got the sack. The affair with the married teacher was complicated by an awful accident on a school trip, he lost his job and so did she and later Adele was named in his divorce. That was the end of her brief teaching career and she ran back to Morrison and he forgave her on the understanding that she never contacted the man again. But it couldn't have been important to her, could it, or she would never have agreed to drop him like a stone? She laughed it off when I asked her what happened to the poor guy. 'I didn't own him, Fifi, how would I know what he did with himself? Anyway, he was a lousy teacher.' I remember those words of hers and I knew then that Adele was never the same girl after that showdown at the school. And she had discovered her sexuality, of course, her power over men. She stayed with Morrison for a bit till the rumpus had died down but there was talk about her entertaining his male students at their house and eventually she just walked out. She refused to discuss the details even with me, said it was a part of her life she wanted to black out entirely. Morrison went to pieces after that. Later, St Francis's offered him a place and he crawled back to Cambridge with his tail between his legs."

"But he never divorced her."

"Never."

"But Underwood wasn't the only one?"

"Gosh no. And I have no idea what happened during her years living in Avignon. We lost touch for a bit but when she moved back to Cambridge and started up this property finding business we homed in on each other as if there had been no intermission. But she *had* changed," she added thoughtfully.

"You never married yourself?"

She laughed. "No-one ever asked me. And you?"

"Got my fingers badly burnt with a wife who later decided she preferred women so I'm clearly no catch. We're divorced now. Still arguing over custody of the cat though."

"I must let you have my card. I'm brilliant at divorce settlements. Adele finally got round to starting divorce proceedings herself you know. Too late," she murmured, frowning at the plate of grilled sole placed before her.

They chatted on amicably while the waitress heaped their table with more dishes but Preston could not resist pressing Fiona for the rest of the story. For some unimaginable reason the character of a woman he had recently seen dissected on a mortuary slab intrigued him, the short life of Adele Morrison gaining rather than losing interest since the case was closed.

"The professor insisted to me that divorce was never an issue between them," he said.

Fiona snorted, dabbing at her mouth with her napkin, grinning across the table at him.

"The old fibber! I'd written to him myself outlining her terms. She never needed to negotiate, I told her that but Adele had got used to making deals, she said it was worth bribing him for a quick settlement. I sometimes wondered if he had some sort of hold over her, refusing her her freedom all these years."

"So, suddenly, out of the blue, she wanted a quickie divorce?"

"Yes, sure. I think being married suited her in a way, kept the wolves at bay, but Larry was a funny one – she almost seemed scared of what he might do. And until someone tempting came along she wasn't bothered too much about being single again."

"How far had these negotiations gone?"

"Unfortunately, not far enough. But she dangled the

farmhouse in Provence under his nose and he fell for it. The final offer."

This last remark struck a chord but he put it aside as she continued, "You realize all this is in confidence, Ian? I just feel so cross that Adele was cheated. There was no intention of handing him *everything*."

"She didn't make a will."

Fiona slammed her fist on the table causing her wine glass to wobble. "No, damn it. For such a streetwise girl she was terribly superstitious. I nagged her about it often enough but at her age making a will was tempting fate she said."

"How wrong can you be? She died anyway."

"Right."

"So the professor copped everything including the silver."

"What?"

"The silver. The cleaner who did for your friend got a call from Morrison. Said he'd come to collect the family silver."

"No! When was this?"

"Not sure. But before she died. Perhaps she said he could have it, they were on speaking terms I assume."

"An armed truce. He wanted to retire. Adele had always held the pursestrings but having to admit the marriage was over stuck in his gullet. He blames Jamie Ferguson still."

"Ferguson?"

"The teacher. The one whose wife divorced him over their affair at that private school. Larry always insisted it was Ferguson's fault, Adele being led astray by an older man."

"Strewth. Talk about pot calling the kettle black!"

"Precisely. Mind you that girl always went to extremes. Either spotty adolescents barely out of school or father figures."

The waitress cleared their plates and they both declined

puddings, ordering coffee straight away, Fiona checking her watch with the air of a lady with a full schedule. Suddenly, she looked up, her eyes glinting spitefully.

"You know what really gets me. Bloody Larry scooping the pool when he was on the brink of being dumped. He's planning to put Bay Tree Cottage up for sale straight away and rumour has it he's applied for a sabbatical. On compassionate grounds," she added, tight-lipped. "Let's hope he's off before Sylvie turns up."

"The sister?"

Fiona nodded. "I phoned her as soon as I heard. She's flying over for the funeral."

"It's fixed?"

"I'm waiting to hear from the bloody widower. He can't escape me. I'm still involved with probate. Sylvie gets nothing of course. Not even Adele's jewellery. Larry insists on having nothing to do with the rest of the family."

"You kept in touch yourself?"

"No. But I met Sylvie as a little girl just before her father died and when she was over here touring a couple of years ago Adele insisted we all met up for a family reunion."

"Ah, 'Ramola'," Preston said with a stab of recollection.

"You saw it?"

"No. I found an old programme at the cottage when I was checking it out. I've still got it, the programme I mean. Sylvie Reynolds is on the cast list – I missed the connection. Is she any good?"

"Well, I'm not much of a theatregoer myself but Sylvie's often in England working. She and Adele were very close once they got together again though you'd never guess they were sisters. Not a bit alike. Sylvie's dark, almost gypsyish – must take after her mother who I never met. Isobel was French as you know."

"No, I didn't know that."

"That's how the girls got to be so fluent, Sylvie much

more so than Adele, Sylvie being bi-lingual from the cradle according to old man Reynolds. He was dotty about his younger daughter. Broke his heart when Isobel left him and took her to Montreal."

"Adele seems to have had a sad life one way and another."

"Who could blame her for concentrating on her career? Her hopes of settling down were fading fast. Under-wood did promise to marry her you know. He lied at the inquest."

"Why didn't you challenge him?"

She shrugged. "I only had her word for it. There was no point in stirring up more mud. It was Underwood's propo-sal that galvanised her into that hasty divorce negotiation with Larry. As it happened he got everything anyway – not just the French farmhouse. Life's a bitch, Ian. Sylvie deserved her share."

They parted in the car park, promising to meet up again at the funeral, Fiona jotting down the attractive inspector's home number in her bulging filofax, pencilling a little heart by his name, her lighthearted shorthand for "dishy".

Ian sauntered back to the car, mulling over yet more unexpected bits of the jigsaw. One phrase kept recurring. Final offer. A common enough term especially in Adele's line of business but the two words stuck in his brain like a fishbone in the throat. Final offer. At last it clicked: the message from Gary on the answer machine in Bay Tree Cottage. What was the name of the guy who Gary Trenchard had given her mobile number to? He racked his brains and was eventually forced to check his notebook as he sat in the car, rifling back through the pages, trying to decipher the scribbled jottings.

"Gotcha!"

Lawrence. A Mr Lawrence. But maybe it wasn't Lawrence, was it? He checked the Morrison file from his briefcase, his fingers moving down the closely typed pages like a sensor.

Full name: Laurence StJohn Morrison, Fellow of St Francis's College, Cambs.

It wasn't a Mr Lawrence at all. The man pestering Adele that weekend was her other half. Was Morrison's the phonecall which Miss Moffatt remembered hearing after Underwood had driven away? Only a jealously obsessive husband would pursue his wife to their honeymoon hotel in the small hours. What had the bloody professor said to her that last time? Had those furious words been the last straw, driven her to escape from her room to the only place where no bitter recriminations could reach her? Had it been Morrison's insults which had indirectly propelled her to her death and not Underwood's as everyone, including Miss Moffatt, had assumed?

Eleven

Preston was due for a fortnight's leave after that week-end and decided to devote the time to some DIY on the house.

Forge Cottage sat at a crossroads just outside the village, near enough to the A146 to make commuting to the police station a matter of twenty minutes at most. The place was pretty run down he had to admit and Samantha and her butch friend must have looked around with derision when they broke in to look for the cat. Funny thing was, despite his bad press, Ian Preston was not a control freak. Left to his own devices he took a philosophical view of the current chaos of his new home, deciding to live on the breadline until he could afford to buy some furniture he really liked.

He had always fancied living in the country and now, being single and in a position to call the shots, he had jumped at the cheap accommodation Forge Cottage offered. The big attraction was the paddock included in the lot together with several ramshackle sheds, a use for which had yet to occur to him. In the meantime, Kenzo was infatuated with the local moggies, refusing to get to grips with his real work of clearing the outbuildings of vermin. Maybe the cat was a townie like himself just playing with straws in the ears to see if he really liked it.

Preston was not much of a handyman and toyed with the idea of getting someone in to reconstruct the kitchen at least. Problem was he was new in the area and the local builder seemed suspiciously reluctant to ally himself to the police. In fact, Preston was happy to let things ride, to give himself time to decide what to do with the place which clearly had not seen a paintbrush for years. At least he was spared Samantha's input: the festooned curtains, the three-piece suite and, worst of all, the little side tables which had seemed to breed in their Ipswich semi.

August had dissolved into September, the rain of the past weeks allowing the leaves an unseasonal bonus before the colours began to change. Even the ash tree outside his verandah was still green, the slyly lenthening shadows of shortening days hardly perceptible. It was a nice enough place and his misgivings about moving to the country were temporarily lulled though he had to admit his forays into Cambridge on the Morrison case had given him pause for thought. But, there again, how could he afford to live in a city like that after Sam had taken him to the cleaners over the divorce settlement?

The result of the inquest on the Morrison girl had come as no surprise but the intriguing details of the case still bothered him. He tried to thrust them aside, to ignore a tic working away in his subconscious that he had not handled the investigation with his usual assiduity. But there was nothing else to go on, was there? And even her best friend, the solicitor woman who had known her since college was firmly of the opinion that suicide was never an option. And she should know. Fiona had probably shared more confidences with the dead woman than anyone and, to be fair, harboured no illusions about her friend's lack of judgment when it came to men.

Marrying Morrison before she was even twenty-one was Adele's first mistake of course. But things went downhill after that through no fault of the professor's who, all those years ago, must have retained a certain sex appeal. The poor bloke just didn't know what he had got himself into. And what about his wife's adultery with the schoolteacher? That had cost the Ferguson fellow his livelihood and his family and Adele had dropped him like a stone. But perhaps this incident on the school trip Fiona Blakestock had mentioned had tipped the scales as far as the school governors were concerned. Perhaps Ferguson's staff room liaison with the pretty young French mistress had not been the only reason he had been sacked. He must remember to ask Fiona more about it when they met.

In fact she rang the very next day, quoting the date and time of Adele Morrison's burial. It was to be held the following week at a crematorium in Cambridge. Fiona expected few mourners, the professor aiming to get it over with maximum privacy. In this hope the widower was out of luck, Fiona taking it upon herself to alert Adele's business colleagues together with any other old friends she could muster.

"Poor girl deserved a decent send off. That miserable sod, Larry, would put her on a bonfire in the garden if he could get away with it, just to keep the rest of us away. Trying to keep Adele to himself was one of his major blunders – she got claustrophobic with all his fussing round. No wonder she ran amok, embarrassed him by frolicking with his own students. Do you think I should leave a message for Underwood? Sylvie wants to meet him, practically insists on it, heaven knows why. She's staying with me at present."

Preston's interest quickened. "The little sister?"

"Not so little now! Thirty at least and making a name for herself at last. On the stage that is. She begins rehearsals for a pre-London run of 'Hedda Gabler' this month."

"Star part?"

"No. Mrs Elvsted or something like that. Don't ask me. You *must* come to the funeral, Ian, she wants to meet you."

"Me?"

"I must warn you though. Sylvie's in a funny frame of

mind. Thinks it was suicide. Nothing I say makes a bit of difference. Wants to discuss the case with you."

"Oh, no!"

"Oh, do come. Please. I'd like to see you again and I've organised a little buffet do at Bracewell's afterwards. Sylvie can't afford a party and Larry refuses to get involved but Adele would have loved a good old booze-up. Come to the party even if you want to sidestep the funeral. Six o'clock. I'll send directions, shall I?"

Ian reluctantly agreed, wondering if it was wise involving himself in a case officially filed away, done and dusted. Still, he was on leave, wasn't he? And meeting the sister was tempting, having always harboured a certain starstruck attraction to life on the boards. Why had he chosen to become a policeman for God's sake? And why, all of a sudden, was he starting to question the path he had chosen? The divorce had shaken him up. And moving from the lively criminal scene in a busy town was a consequence of that. He sighed. Must be a mid-life crisis, he jeered at himself as he finished speaking with the Blakestock girl and put down the phone.

He skipped the crematorium and drove straight to the wake. Fiona had hired a room above a shop in Trumpington Street and had got plenty of food and wine in, a catered affair already in full throttle when he arrived. He recognised a few faces: Gary Trenchard gave a wave from across the room and the amber-eyed receptionist from Frobisher & Kent came over to say hello. She had perked up since the news of Adele's death had seasoned, and Preston hoped that a tender-hearted soul such as she had also excused herself from the funeral. The room was crowded, the air thick with cigarette smoke and music, probably just the sort of party Adele Morrison would have revelled in. It seemed unimportant that everyone was dressed in mourning.

Fiona pushed her way through the crowd to greet him,

dragging a waiter with a tray of wine glasses in her wake and thrusting a full-bodied burgundy in his hand.

"Don't stint yourself, Ian. Gary's offered his house for crashing out, save you driving home."

"Very generous of him, Fiona. An impressive tribute you've laid on here."

"Least I could do."

"Did the funeral pass off OK? No gatecrashers?"

"Only us. Larry got so cross seeing all Adele's friends filling the chapel he forgot to look tearful."

He grinned. "You're an unforgiving girl, Fiona."

"Larry Morrison ruined her life. I've said it before and I'll die with it on my lips so get used to it, Inspector. Anyway, raise your glass to the poor absentee, she would have loved a bash like this."

He did as he was bid, his eyes alighting on a tall female who had taken Fiona's elbow. She spun round.

"Ah, Sylvie. Thought we'd lost you. Let me introduce Ian Preston."

The girl was dark, very dark; her hair and eyes and olive skin setting her apart in this braying crush of English people. She wore an amethyst silk tunic over fishnet tights. No make-up apart from kohl-rimmed eyes, and, as she held out her hand, Ian Preston felt a distinct frisson, almost of recognition. He had been told Sylvie was different from her sister but the truth was unbelievable. No wonder the late Mr Reynolds had been besotted about his two beautiful daughters, the sun and moon of his existence.

"I need to talk to you," she insisted, giving Fiona a gentle shove. "Excuse us, darling, but this man is on my hit list."

"Wow! Get you," Fiona chortled, grabbing the waiter as he moved in on them again, this time with canapes, and taking the tray from him she disappeared in the cluster of guests milling around Gary Trenchard who was, unbelievably, doing card tricks at the bar.

Ian found himself drawn away.

"Have you had enough of this?" she said.

"Have a heart. I've only just arrived!"

"I know. But you weren't a friend of my sister's, were you? Fiona won't mind. I've flown all the way from Canada to settle this business in my mind. Refused a chance with a Shakespeare run just to talk to you, Ian Preston," she said, smiling.

He drew back, wondering if this femme fatale gene ran in the blood of these two sisters. He laughed nervously, sipping his wine, feeling a bit of a berk to tell the truth.

Sylvie's smile faded. "I'm serious. There's so much I don't know. Won't you help me? Let's go back to your place. I know there were things which didn't come out at the inquest. We could run through it together. It would give me something to go on."

"The case is closed, Sylvie. Let it rest."

"I can't," she whispered, the kohl-rimmed eyes brimming.

He steered her outside and tried to reason with her but it was no good.

Finally, he gave in.

Twelve

They hardly spoke on the drive back, Sylvie actually dozing off during his back-route which bypassed Bury St Edmunds. Preston grew pensive, increasingly worried at the turn events had taken. This sister of the dead girl was only going to aggravate his own misgivings about the case and what would that achieve for either of them?

She seemed unfazed by the shambles Forge Cottage presented, presumably used to theatrical digs of doubtful comfort. Although unquestionably beautiful and oddly spellbinding – what with her sepia-toned voice and the eyes of an houri – her manner was unaffected and when she giggled even the cat was bowled over, jumping on to her lap as Ian poured the drinks.

"Bloody animal usually runs a mile from strangers. Specially women. Couldn't stand my ex-wife funnily enough though she was the one to give him that stupid name."

"Kenzo? I like it. Sounds expensive."

"Anything's upmarket for a ginger tom."

He settled in his scarred leather armchair smiling at this unexpected visitor silhouetted against the last rays of sunset glimmering through the uncurtained window behind her head.

"You're worried about this, aren't you?" she said.

He nodded. "I never met your sister, of course. Anything I have to tell you would merely be the bare facts assembled for the inquest."

"But it wasn't an accident."

"Of course it was."

"Adele wasn't the sort to die in error."

"That's a funny way of putting it. You think she was murdered?"

Sylvie shrugged, stroking the cat asleep on her lap which in the gloaming seemed merely a dead bundle of fur, only the strong reverberations of purring saying otherwise.

Preston patiently reiterated his argument. "There's no evidence, nothing whatsoever, to put anyone else on the scene. Her hotel room was locked. No-one could kidnap her and frogmarch her down to the pool area – the woman in the next room had her ears flapping, would have heard any intruder breaking in through the fire exit via their shared balcony and dragging her down in the lift."

"Suppose he had a knife? Forced her."

"Down to the basement? No sound? No wounds? Believe me, Sylvie, that girl went voluntarily, on her own, following a row with her roommate. You don't know it all. Shall I go over it in detail with you? You weren't at the inquest and the reports in the local press were far from accurate. The general public wasn't interested – an accidental drowning doesn't rate so much as a paragraph in the nationals unless you're a TV star or something. I tell you what – I'll knock up some supper for us and if you promise to put Adele off limits for an hour I'll give you everything you need to know to put your mind at rest. Stay here, I'll open another bottle and we'll lay your ghost for good."

He put on a couple of lamps which gave the starkness of the unfurnished room a glow of comfort and closed the door on her. Certainly a poor handyman but Preston's ability with a jumbo frying pan was in a different class altogether, having had years of practice when policework had kept him out all hours and Samantha's wifely duties ran under strictly feminist trade union rules.

He rustled up a risotto and assembled a platter of cheese

on a decent serving board for once. Sylvie was impressed and Kenzo, sniffing the steaming chicken and prawns, perked up immediately. Preston put a match to the firewood in the grate and they ate in front of the blazing dry faggots he had found piled up in the blacksmith's workshop. The wine weaved its magic and they were soon as cosy as a pair of old slippers side by side at the hearth.

"Tell me about your current tour. 'Hedda Gabler', Fiona seemed to think."

"A rehash of a run we had in the States a couple of years ago. A group of us sometimes make a foray with an old favourite, something people know and love," she added with a moue. "We have all worked together before – it's like family. There's not much money in it but we're each hoping to be 'discovered' overnight, making headlines in the weekend supplements. To be honest I only wangled myself into this run of 'Hedda' at the last minute. I needed to get my head round Adele's death. It doesn't make sense to me. It still doesn't. And I couldn't afford to stop working."

"You're rehearsing right now?"

"Yes. At a grotty church hall in Barons Court. Then we get a week in a small theatre in Battersea followed by a string of secondary venues in the provinces. In the course of the run our producer is trying to mobilise a contract for us in Edinburgh or Birmingham next year."

"It's a Canadian ensemble?"

"A very mixed bag. It's called Garnett's Rep – after the guy who set it up. We were in drama school together. We shacked up in New York for a couple of years but it didn't work out."

"But you still manage to work together?"

"Yes, of course. Why not?"

"Well that sister of yours never learned the knack."

She bridled. "What do you mean by that?"

He raised an index finger. "Lover number one, Professor

81

Morrison. Relationship ditched and he remains bitter to this day blaming lover number two," he said, raising a second finger, "another teacher, a man called James Ferguson who lost his job following the scandal of his and Adele's relationship which was subsequently cited by his wife in their divorce. Then, to top it all, he was promptly dumped and presumably never forgave her. And three," he continued, putting up a third digit, "poor bloody Underwood who, for the price of a bit of fun on the side, found himself publicly outed at the inquest, dubbed a cad of the old school by every woman in the courtroom for having had the temerity to walk out on your sister when she trashed the hotel room around him as he tried to make a decent exit."

"A decent exit?" she shrilled. "The man pretended he was going to buy a country house through her business, promised to marry her and then walked out in the middle of the night probably leaving the bill unpaid."

"Ah, no, you're wrong there. Underwood paid in cash, in advance, and even tipped the garden boy on his way out."

"You mean that pool attendant? Simon Harris? What was he doing? Helping Underwood to make a quick getaway?"

He collapsed in laughter, pulling her to him, kissing her nose as she struggled in his arms.

"Hey, cool it! I was teasing. I apologise. It's no laughing matter – terribly poor taste. Forgive me?"

She relaxed a little and, emboldened, Preston continued.

"As a matter of fact that boy was the exception in the Hate Adele Brigade. He had an adolescent crush on her himself years before when he was a student in Cambridge. He was jettisoned just like the big boys but held no grudges. Extraordinary coincidence him finding the body though."

"I don't believe in coincidences."

"In my business, lady, you'd be surprised how often they crop up."

Sylvie looked sceptical but at least the glint of battle in her eye had burnt out and, pushing him away, she collected up their plates and dumped them in the kitchen. He heard her filling the kettle and lit a cigarette, knowing all too well that this particular dark lady of the sonnets was not going to release him from his promise to sift every grain of sand in this gritty case.

After coffee they settled down to go through Preston's notes on the Morrison enquiry. He insisted on no interruption while he detailed every stage of his investigation and after finally giving a resume of the inquest he put his feet up on a wooden beer crate he had discovered in the outhouse and which, in the absence of anything more genteel, temporarily served as a coffee table.

Sylvie lay stretched out on the sofa, her eyes closed. In the silence the ticking of the clock marked some sort of conclusion. At last she looked across at him as if from a long, long way off.

"I'm sorry, Ian. But I'm not convinced. If everything denies the possibility of someone being there, feeding her some drug or knock-out pill to cause her to black out later in the water, then it was suicide."

He leapt up, suddenly angry. "Bloody hell, Sylvie, of all the rot I've heard in the course of years with villains who wouldn't know the truth if they fell over it, that just about takes the biscuit. The Home Office pathologist practically rinsed her innards through a colander and certainly examined every inch of flesh. Do hard facts mean nothing to you? I suppose," he spat, "you're saying it's women's intuition. Well, leave me out of it."

She raised herself on her elbow and looked him straight in the eye.

"OK. I'll do it on my own. And I'll start by tracking down lover number three as you call him, Underwood. Then I'll work back to lover number two, Ferguson, wasn't it? And eventually I'll get back to bedrock and put that horrible man Morrison through the mill and check out his phony alibi for the night she died."

"Don't forget the boy who cleaned the swimming pool, not to mention Uncle Tom Cobbleigh and All who dallied with that sex-crazed sister of yours."

"Good thinking, Inspector Preston. Now call me a minicab so I can go home."

His anger suddenly fizzled out and he grabbed her arm, murmuring insistent apologies for his bull-headedness.

"Stay, Sylvie. Please. No strings. You can even share my bed with Kenzo. I'll make up the couch. And tomorrow, scout's honour, we'll drive to London together and see what Underwood's got to say for himself."

But as it happened they never got that far.

Next morning the phone shrilled before either of them was awake. Sylvie awoke with a start and stumbled into the sitting room as Preston rolled off the sofa, rubbing his chin as he moved across to the grimy phone screwed to the wall.

He stiffened, suddenly awake, his unseeing eyes seemingly boring into the girl hovering in the doorway draped in a towel. His response to the caller was terse, his manner brusque in the extreme. Sylvie felt uncomfortable and turned away to get dressed, confused by this sudden change of mood.

Frowning, he made a rush for the stairs, and then swivelled round as if suddenly remembering he was not alone.

"I'll drop you at the station," he said.

She stared, openmouthed.

He drew a deep breath, carefully framing his words. "Look, I'm sorry about all this but something's cropped up. My leave's cancelled. I've got to go into work straight away."

Her face hardened and she turned away. As if deciding to come clean, Preston moved back into the room to pull her back, knowing it would only be a matter of time before she knew everything anyway.

"There's been a development," he said thickly. "You can forget about Adele's lover number two. He's featured in someone's hit list already."

"Underwood's dead?"

"No. Ferguson. James Ferguson, lover number two, remember?"

"What happened?"

"He was mugged on Hungerford Bridge late last night and thrown into the Thames."

"They caught the muggers?"

"A group of drunks was lounging at the end of the walkway after a pub crawl in Soho. They reckon they saw two men talking together, leaning over the rail. There was a scuffle and Ferguson was hoisted over the side – his body was later recovered by the river police several miles downstream."

"The killer got away?"

"Ran off and disappeared in the dark. The boozers were too far gone to give chase, all but legless apparently."

"What's it to do with you, a mugging in London?"

"Ferguson had an envelope in his pocket stuffed with press cuttings reporting your sister's drowning together with a tagged key for room sixteen at the Swan House Hotel. They're sending someone here to check out the Morrison enquiry – the case will be taken apart all over again. This time it's linked with a murder enquiry."

She sank on to the sofa clutching the towel with shaking fingers. "I'll come with you, Ian – I can't go back to rehearsals now."

He grabbed her arms, crouching in front of this woman whom he had barely met, knowing it was vital to keep her at a distance until the smoke had cleared.

"Go. For God's sake, Sylvie, get away from here before you get caught up in it too. There's something evil going on and I have to work it out on my own. I promise, swear to you, that I'll bring you back here as soon as I've cleared up this mess. Have you got a contact number?"

Within ten minutes they were roaring out of the village towards the Intercity rail pick-up at Diss. Sylvie, temporarily bulldozed into accepting Preston's urgent appeal, reluctantly found herself shoved back to the land of theatrical makebelieve, only half convinced of Preston's motives.

Thirteen

S ylvie was late for rehearsal, a fact which she got away with as the director was going hammer and tongs at the leading man. The row was on the lines of "Now we can do this the easy way or the hard way" which in a workshop situation is guaranteed to put the entire cast on the defensive.

The director, a Scot called Rennie Coles, was new to the Garnett Rep and a bonehead unfamiliar with the antagonism generated when a director acts out a part himself, particularly if, as in this case, the troop had worked together before.

Sylvie slipped into a seat at the back of the hall and lit a cigarette. Her hand shook as she extinguished the match, the trauma of Adele's death and subsequent swift despatch insistently inserting itself between her attempts to concentrate on the rehearsal. Joanna Attwell, the girl playing Hedda, dropped into the seat beside her and cadged a cigarette.

"Sorry to hear about your sister, Sylv. Harry told me what happened. What a ghastly thing. Poor you."

Sylvie pressed the girl's hand, snatching a glance at the new leading lady beside her before returning her attention to the stage.

"Yeah. I'm doing my damnedest to shake it off but there were complications. Let's not talk about it, Jo. Tell me, how's this Rennie Coles shaping up?"

"Harry's worried about him. Trouble is most of the

cast, like yourself, have done Ibsen before. Obviously, Rennie wants to put his own stamp on it but Garnett's has a reputation as an actors' workshop, and because we're so short of rehearsal time, new kids like me are finding it hard fitting in with a group that can practically sleepwalk through the entire production. You played Hedda with Garnett's in New York last time, didn't you?"

Sylvie nodded.

"Do you mind taking Elvsted? It's such a small part. My understudy, Eve, thought she'd bagged it herself before you came along."

Sylvie grinned. "Rotten luck. Strictly between ourselves, I pulled strings to get this part. Standard procedure: I slept with the producer."

"Harry?" she squealed.

"A while ago now. Harry Garnett and I were an item for a couple of years but it wore off. Nothing acrimonious. We just got bored with each other."

"Why on earth did you want this part? I freaked out when I heard you were replacing Eve as Elvsted – me who's never even been to Europe before playing opposite someone who knows the role backwards. Don't you mind?"

Sylvie smiled grimly, grinding her cigarette into the dusty floorboards. "Nice to be a backseat driver for once. Honestly, Joanna, you're going to be marvellous – it's a terrific chance to make a name for yourself and I've got other things on my mind just now. Has Rennie posted a rehearsal schedule yet? I need to work round it."

"We're doing our big scene after lunch."

"The one where Hedda is so insufferably condescending to Mrs Elvsted?"

"Mm. I thought we could have a chat about it while Rennie's putting Charles through the mincer. I've got a few ideas of my own. Fancy a coffee?"

They sneaked out through a side exit and found a cafe in the next street, leaving a message with the caretaker just to make the director feel wanted. The rehearsal ground on throughout the evening and it was almost ten before Sylvie got back to her digs.

The boarding house in Brixton was a familiar stop-off for Sylvie and two other actors from Garnett's. The proprietor, an old queen called Leslie, kept open house, producing a greasy fry-up into the small hours for his everchanging clientele, breakfast being more of a self-help operation which his regulars mostly chose to avoid. Leslie had been something of a chart topper in the seventies, a lead guitarist before boy bands took over. Much professional heart-searching swilled round the post-performance piss-ups which inevitably cranked into top gear after midnight, the actors taking an unspoken precedence over the rag bag of musicians and aging chorus boys who gravitated to Leslie's like fools' gold in a pan of silt.

Sylvie could afford something better, something cleaner and certainly something more upmarket than the Dossers' Palace as Harry Garnett called it. But Sylvie could relax in Leslie's smoke-filled back room, collapsing into one of his broken-down sofas after a performance like a hedgehog into a warm compost heap. It was the only bolthole where she knew she could push away the insistent fear that Adele's death was only the beginning. Something evil, which even that policeman Ian Preston could perceive, drifted from Adele's grave like an unquiet spirit, urging her on.

The nightly get-together was already starting to group round Leslie's gas fire when Sylvie got back, mostly under-employed session musicians judging from the chat. The room was dim as a cavern, pulsing with the insistent rhythm of one of Leslie's old hits, the air heavy with unfulfilled hopes. At the end of the room a blousy female decked out in a sequinned turban and with a gravity-defying decolletage mimed the lyrics, gesticulating suggestively with talon-like false fingernails, eyelashes flapping away like furry car wash rollers as she hammered it up. The gang was loving every minute, even Leslie who harboured no sensitivities about the desecration of the disc which had financed the unmortgaged boarding house. As her eyes familiarised with the dense atmosphere, Sylvie joined in the applause, helping herself from the percolator Leslie kept bubbling away like a hookah in the hearth. "She" was a drag artist, of course, the heavy make-up tragically exaggerating the manly features the guy was at pains to camouflage.

Leslie came over and kissed her cheek. "Bite to eat, Sylvie, love? Nice bit of gammon in the oven."

"No thanks, Leslie. It's been a long day. Any calls for me?"

He shook his head, nodding towards a clapped-out comedian with dyed red hair who Sylvie seemed to remember from last time. "Kevin's been listening out for you all day," he said pointing to the bloke in the turban.

"Been here long?"

"Eight or nine years. Terrific cook and lovely with it," he smirked.

"How come I've missed him when I've stayed here before?"

"Up till Christmas Kev worked late every night at Kelly's Klub. It's only since his day job kicked in he's cut down on the cabaret. Tarot readings – rents a place up west."

"But he's still permanent here?"

Leslie let out a loud guffaw. "Till my next rose of summer blooms, sweetie."

Sylvie grinned, poking him in the ribs as she pushed past, taking her mug of coffee upstairs with her. Leslie had turfed out one of the regulars to give Sylvie the first floor front room. "Best room in the house," he had insisted when she arrived back that morning, smoothing the pink duvet with fingers heavy with gold rings like a knuckleduster.

Rewind

Sylvie poured herself a nightcap from the hip flask in her bag and lay on the bed trying to extract some sense from the growing self-criticism of her delay in flying to London when she had heard about Adele. Wasting precious time fixing up this gig with Garnett's was pure miserly procrastination. *I could have borrowed the fare from Maman*, she reflected, *been on the spot for the inquest, formed some sensible conclusions of my own about Adele's crazy lifestyle*. But begging a loan from Isobel would have invited biting recriminations, an innate jealousy of any affection between the two girls festered any conversation about her step-daughter, a girl she had never taken to even at the start. Isobel Reynolds had left England with Sylvie determined to sever all contact with her past, but Reynolds' death had brought them together over the will and afterwards Adele had secretly written to her little sister at boarding school, a subterfuge Isobel Schurrer, as she now was, found impossible to forgive.

Sylvie had a leisurely bath, renewing the hot water from Leslie's ancient geyser, trying to remember all the fancy moves in her double act with the new girl playing Hedda. She wondered if playing second fiddle was something she would have to get used to. Time for stardom was running out. Getting rave reviews for Garnett's new production would require one hell of a PR exercise. Anything short of doing the bloody play in the buff Sylvie knew, in her bones, would prove a turkey.

She tried to snuggle down under the duvet but the room was stuffy, the airlessness close as a prison cell. Opening the window would be a mistake, car horns and traffic noise trailing on, as she well knew, far into the night.

She switched on the light. Only twelve-thirty and her brain, jumpy with exhaustion, refused to lie down. Putting on her kimono, she padded down the landing to the payphone, muted shouts of laughter rising from Leslie's little house party in the front room downstairs.

"Hi, it's me. Sylvie."

Preston sighed, slumping in the leather armchair like a deflating tyre.

"Did I wake you, Ian?"

"No such luck."

"Any news?"

"Having dragged me back to that bloody hotel at day-break, the inspector they'd sent down to run through the reports didn't show her face till three."

"A woman?"

"Some cow from the Met. You'd think they'd have enough to do."

"How did Ferguson get hold of Adele's hotel key?"

"Search me."

"And the press cuttings. Surely they'd have been reduced to pulp by the time they fished him out of the river."

"They were stashed into a plastic bag. The DI had had them dried out. Not that anyone should be surprised the poor sap had kept tabs on the woman who had ruined his life."

"What was Ferguson doing in London?"

"Apparently he part-owned a restaurant in Waterloo called 'Le Pendu'. Not exactly a three star place but handy for the South Bank crowd."

"But if the mugger took his wallet how was Ferguson so quickly identified?"

"Actually, he wasn't robbed. I saw a list of the contents of his pockets."

"And the hotel key's genuine?"

"Absolutely kosher. It might have been sent to him through the post to link him with Adele right up to the end or he may have really been there that night so discounting the general impression that they'd not seen each other for years. But there was a mix-up the stupid receptionist admitted to eventually. I'll explain later. Did Adele ever mention Ferguson to you?"

"Before my time."

Preston sighed, wishing now he had kept Sylvie with him at the cottage, the low timbre of her voice echoing in the skimpily carpeted landing of the boarding house as seductive as a siren's song.

"Was there anything else in his pockets? Any letters from Adele? Her phone number?"

"Zilch. One small thing bugs me though. Your sister was allegedly very superstitious. A bouquet of white heather which she may have bought for herself was in the hotel room. Know anything about it?"

"White heather? For luck?"

"Suppose so."

Sylvie frowned. "Actors are notoriously silly about lucky charms, taboo phrases, whistling in the dressing room, all that sort of thing. But Adele? Frankly, I would have said she was the last to touch wood. What's worrying you?"

"Only that this chap Ferguson had a bunch of white heather in his back pocket, a buttonhole. The sort of thing you get forced into buying from gypsies blocking the door at Harrods."

"So what?"

"Oh nothing. Just seemed curious to me. Men's intuition," he added bleakly. "Look, get some sleep, Sylvie. I'll ring you tomorrow night."

"Promise?"

"Sure. Any hope of you getting the weekend off?"

"Not the way the new director's playing it."

"Pity. If I can pack up this re-investigation by Sunday I'll drive up, shall I? Drag you off by your hair."

"Wow! Caveman talk. I love it."

Fourteen

Detective Inspector Rachel Wilkinson had no qualms about driving Swan House's receptionist, Tracey, down to the station and placing her in an interview room, the unfortunate girl cooling her heels for a further half an hour waiting for the door to reopen. Preston insisted on being present, and, armed with Tracey's original statement, sat in on the tearful regurgitation of the saga of the missing key.

Following the usual preliminaries, the D.I. from London kicked in with no more delay. Rachel Wilkinson was actually rather attractive Preston admitted, if the bossy type appealed to you that was. She was below average height and wore little make-up, the attraction resting on a direct blue gaze and a lively turn of phrase. Her hair was fair and unruly, cut close to her head, one ear pierced with a row of gold rings, an adornment seeming totally off target if the impression she was bent on presenting was that of an establishment police officer tipped for the top.

"Now, can we take it from the beginning, Miss Lovelace? Mr Underwood booked two double rooms, numbers sixteen and eighteen, in person and paid in cash in advance."

Tracey nodded, blowing her nose.

"Please answer yes or no."

"Yes."

"When they arrived on the tenth of August he was accompanied by Mrs Morrison, the deceased."

"No. They came separately. In their own cars."

"I see. And the gentleman signed in using his business address in London?"

"Yes."

"And gave no credit card details?"

"I told all this to the sergeant," she said, rallying a little.

The D.I. smiled, revealing small even teeth, and Preston tensed, feeling some sympathy with Tracey who would, he knew, never win against Wilkinson's interviewing technique honed presumably in the torture chambers which passed as interview rooms where she came from.

"OK. Let's skip the obvious and get down to basics shall we, Miss Lovelace? Everything went according to plan until Mr Underwood checked out early. Right?"

Tracey nodded, quickly mouthing a sulky "Yeah" before Wilkinson could tap her wrist again about verbalising for the recording.

"He left during the night?" the inspector persisted.

"How would I know?"

"Fair enough. Let's say we *presume* he left about one thirty say when no-one was on duty in the office. No night porter?"

"Not in the summer. The main door's locked at ten off season and Tim Mason from the village does a night shift from October till Easter but when the place is full of young people coming and going all hours from Yarmouth and up the coast Mrs Mayo don't bother. The guests are always losing keys and the owner, she don't want the expense of keeping a night porter on all year or providing all the summer people with front door keys."

"Not very security conscious the owner then?"

"More a question of being tightfisted if you ask me."

"You get a different type of clientele in the winter?"

"Course we do. Stands to reason, don't it?"

"What's the attraction up the coast then? Shows?"

"Ain't you never been to Yarmouth in August?" Tracey

retorted, genuinely confused. Preston grinned, feeling it was time he put in a word, seeing as the D.I. who had come all the way from London to check on the bloody hotel key was patiently losing all credibility with the locals having already been rebuffed by the pool attendant, Simon Harris, who refused to alter his original statement by so much as a comma.

"Great Yarmouth and, to a lesser extent, Lowestoft offer a whole range of family entertainments and discos in the season, mostly catering for popular tastes. Southwold's just a few miles up the road but has a more genteel image, appeals more to notions of what beach holidays used to be about. I'll take you for a drive round if you like, give you the feel of the place and . . ."

"No thanks," she snapped, tapping the file with her biro. "Let's get back to business, shall we?"

Preston grinned at Tracey, hoping to spur her on to kick this particular ball into touch before the whistle blew on both of them.

"Right. So doors were left unlocked all round the place and before Mr Underwood left he went into your office and left an envelope addressed to Mrs Mayo tucked inside the visitors' book."

"Yeah. Like I said. He left a wodge for the bar bill and extra for tips."

"And his key?"

"That's right. Mrs Mayo and me was just sorting it out when the police arrived. Simon had rung 999 without telling her first. It all got a bit confusing after that," she added with a defiant lift of her chin. Preston noticed that the girl's eyes were still red, the mascara scrubbed way off target during her agonising wait for the inter- view to begin, an unnecessary tactic in his view, the kid was hardly any sort of experienced villain rehearsing an alibi.

"But you originally stated he left the key for room

sixteen, didn't you, Miss Lovelace? And that wasn't true, was it?"

Tracey's eyes narrowed, a chip of obduracy hardening her response. "Did I? Well, we was all at sixes and sevens, wasn't we? Mr Underwood paid the bill for number sixteen, he slept in number sixteen and must have been using the key for number sixteen so stands to reason, dunnit? Mrs Mayo and me checked the cash and one of us, I forget who, hung the key back on the board with all the others like always. Didn't give it much thought at the time what with him and his lot," she said, nodding at Preston, "buzzing about like bluebottles, getting everyone in a state. Not every day we get a corpse on the premises," she said acidly.

Preston intervened. "I must put in a word for Tracey here, Inspector. Sunday morning, before breakfast, is no time to be on the ball in this little backwater of ours. It may be that some members of my team were inconsiderate."

The woman eyed him speculatively, weighing up the marginally defensive attitude this colleague seemed to be adopting.

"Maybe you and your team may live to regret that, Inspector Preston."

She turned back to Tracey, refocussing her aim.

"When did you realise that the key Mr Underwood handed in was the key to room eighteen, the room he was allocated in the original booking?"

"Last Tuesday," she retorted.

"Why did it take you so long?"

"There weren't no problem with the keys. She asked for an extra key for her friend when she arrived 'cos they were going to be working in her room she said and I thought nothing of it. Why should I? Number sixteen weren't rebooked till September – Mrs Mayo felt bad about it, said it had bad vibes. So we left it empty after the police had finished with it. There wasn't much in the way of late bookings and once the kids are back at school the take-up thins out. We generally give all the rooms a bit of a going over before the oldies start pouring in after the summer tariff comes down and the autumn breaks kick in."

"Where were the keys all this time?"

"Mrs Mayo didn't get them back for ages. He," she said, pointing at Preston, "took them, the keys for sixteen *and* eighteen we thought, and by the time they was returned and I told Mrs Mayo that we was short, we sort of assumed the police had lost one lot. We only got back the housekeeper's key and the one Mrs Morrison had in her room."

Her interrogator swung round on Preston, hawk-eyed.

"No receipts?"

He shrugged, trying to look as nonplussed as herself. In truth he couldn't remember. In truth, looking back on that apparently unremarkable drowning accident he *had* been a little remiss about the bloody investigation.

She turned back on the hapless Tracey.

"What then?"

"I told Mrs Mayo I'd get on to the nice sergeant and get him to poke about in drawers or wherever they keep this sort of stuff. But Mrs Mayo was dead against it – didn't want nothin' more to do with the police, said she'd sort it out herself."

"She got an extra key cut."

Tracey nodded. "Every season we lose a few – people forget to hand them in and phoning round trying to get them back's been such a palaver in the past that we just get the missing lot replaced at the end of the season. In Lowestoft," she said, the address tripping off her tongue like a well-practised mantra. "We only got the bill yesterday. Six keys all replaced ready for another year."

"Tags too?"

"Complete service. Quick and cheap. Why don't you ask Mrs Mayo all this? She was the one who organised it."

"I will. Do you remember the numbers?"

"What numbers?"

"The room numbers of the keys that had to be replaced?"

"Course I don't. D'you think I'm a bloody mastermind? Can I go now?"

"Just sit here, Miss Lovelace, while I get your statement typed up. Here's a pen, make it snappy and you can be off in a panda car."

Later when they were alone, Preston watched his new collaborator skim through the mountain of paper appertaining to the Morrison case.

"Any brainwaves?"

"Anyone could have pinched Underwood's key from their room, the fire exit wasn't bolted up. She could even have given it to someone else – the pool attendant for instance, inviting him up after her swim. It's already established that he knew she was alone, no reason why he didn't ring her up and suggest a tete-a-tete, especially as they were already well acquainted from his Cambridge days you said."

"He could have accessed number sixteen via the fire escape but so could anyone else – it was a hot night and she wasn't coy about pulling the curtains, silly bitch. But why would Simon need a key? Last thing he'd want, to be seen *inside* the hotel in the small hours."

"Who's to see him?"

Preston laughed. "Get real, Inspector, the risk would be too great, he'd be out on his ear if someone like Miss Moffatt saw him bowling down the corridor."

She made a grimace. "This Miss Moffatt was the lady who heard Morrison's mobile phone ringing in the next room after Underwood drove off?"

"That's the one."

"Her address?"

"In the file though you might have a long trek. She does trans-continental bicycle rides when she's not got her ear shoved up to the wall in seaside hotels. Does lectures too. I reckon Miss Moffatt's the sort who doesn't do much sitting at home watching TV in her retirement. Anyway, we still don't know how Ferguson got hold of the key, do we?"

She pressed on, changing tack, slippery as an eel when it came to awkward questions. "And this bloke Underwood. I can't get hold of him at this address in SW11 he gave on the booking form."

"Another one who travels a lot. He's a dealer. In books."

She scrawled a large question mark against the name and looked up, tapping her pen on the open file.

"You've spelt his name wrong."

"What?"

"Underwood's name. It's given here as Brendon with an 'o'. It's spelt B.R.E.N.D.A.N. It's an old Irish name – Brendan. Like Behan, the playwright."

Preston grabbed the file from her, sparking dangerously. "Mine's right. Look here in the inquest report. Brendon with an 'o' and he's signed it himself."

She ran her finger down the typed sheet and finally let him have the point.

"OK. You win. But it's an odd spelling, especially as his surname's Underwood. You've never been there?"

"Where?"

"Grendon Underwood, near Aylesbury. There's a prison there where they do marvellous work. Group therapy, counselling the inmates – all that sort of thing. I did a course there once."

"Grendon?"

"Yes. But Brendon's pretty close, isn't it? Perhaps his mother worked there, supported this idea of therapy through volunteers who agree to open up to their fellow prisoners. Interesting treatment – doesn't always work, of course, a proportion reoffend."

"Underwood's middle aged, any christening obviously predated this place by decades," he jeered.

"Just a thought. Lateral thinking it's called."

Preston slammed his file shut and stalked out, weary to death with the woman's nitpicking methods, painfully conscious of the very same criticisms which had been levelled at him before he transferred from Ipswich. No doubt about it, the country air must have had a numbing effect. He would never have left the Morrison case with so many loopholes six months ago.

Fifteen

Preston telephoned Sylvie that evening after she got back from rehearsals. It took three attempts, contact eventually being made almost at midnight. Sylvie admitted that rehearsals had not really been going on that long but, after another six rounds slogging it out with the new director, the nucleus of Garnett's Rep got together in a pizza place after shut-down at Barons Court to cobble together some sort of joint protest with which to confront the producer the next day.

"Will you speak for us, Sylvie?"

She drew back. "Must I? Harry'll only think I'm being tiresome because I can't bear seeing Joanna doing things differently. Look, guys, Harry only gave me this part at the last minute as a favour. I really don't want to end up the scapegoat in all this."

"That's pretty selfish of you if I may say so, Sylvie. What about the rest of us? You know, and Harry knows, that Rennie's fucking up this whole production and we'll all end up with stinking reviews if something's not pulled out of the hat before it's too late."

After more argy-bargy on the same lines, Sylvie reluctantly agreed to be spokesperson and the rest of the evening was spent knocking out a summary of their criticism.

Speaking with Preston that night was almost a relief, the man clearly all too fired up with his own troubles to worry about hers. Ferguson's apparently continuous relationship with Adele was something of a facer for both of them, a relationship Sylvie had never even entered into the equation of her sister's confusing love affairs.

"Ian, I'm thinking of hiring a car. I can't stand the Tube a moment longer and taxis are costing me a bomb. I thought we might meet half way – say Cambridge? I've got a few things to pick up from Fiona's place. If I drive down maybe we could shoehorn it in between shifts?" Her tone was carefully level but to Preston it was music in his ears.

"Shall I book a couple of rooms for us somewhere? Or were you planning a sleep-in at Fiona's?"

"We need to talk. These late-night conversations are driving me crazy. Do you realise I have to take your calls from Leslie's lousy top landing?"

"Get a mobile."

"Ian! I barely have time to wash my hair the way things are running here. But you're right. I'll fix something up when I get the car. When do you think you can get the night off?"

"Friday?"

"Sure, why not? By the time I've had my showdown with our producer in the morning I'll probably be out of a job anyway. Ring me at lunchtime tomorrow – here's the number of the rehearsal room," she said, rattling it off from a reminder penned on the back of her hand.

Next morning she was up early having bagged first option on the bathroom off her first floor landing. En suite facilities did not feature in Leslie's bed-sits and, when in London, Sylvie mostly appealed to the good nature of theatrical friends with their own flats though, in fact, Leslie's bathrooms were not that bad: always plenty of hot water and clean towels. It was the niggling anxiety about the hygiene of her fellow boarders which bugged her.

Leslie's current boyfriend, Kevin, was already in the kitchen when she stepped in. From the back his slight figure bundled up in a candlewick dressing gown plus the inevitable turban looked quite mumsy and, as she hesitated in the doorway, he turned from the cooker and smiled. A very sweet smile, utterly unaffected and not in the least camp.

"I'm doing scrambled eggs. Want some? Nobody gets down here till after eight."

"Sounds terrific."

Sylvie slipped on to the bench seat flanking Leslie's ginormous kitchen table, the scene of nightly pig-ins by the itinerant luvvies.

Kevin worked deftly, his green lacquered fingernails flickering over the hob like humming birds. He placed a creamy dish of eggs on toast in front of her, slapping down a second plate for himself and bringing up a small pot of coffee and a pair of china mugs to complete the repast.

"Gee, this looks wonderful."

"Scrambled eggs need love. A little cream and a gentle poaching does it. Most people turn eggs into rubber gloves."

In the pale light filtering through the window which overlooked the area steps, he looked little more than a teenager in the absence of the obscene make-up. If it hadn't been for the emerald nails and the turban, the scrubbed cheeks of Leslie's right-hand man would have passed muster in the staff room of a prep school.

"Ever thought of training to be a chef?" Sylvie ventured. "You could easily get a place at catering college."

His eyes lit up. "You reckon?"

"No problem. Chefs earn terrific money these days – especially in London. What do you do?"

"My day job you mean?" he said with a faint smile.

Sylvie flushed, feeling herself on dodgy ground here. But he seemed unembarrassed and continued without pause.

"I do tarot readings in Soho. A place over a magic shop. Sells crystals, psychic stuff, you know . . ."

"Really? I've always wanted to have my palm read but

never plucked up the courage. You really go for all this tarot stuff?"

He held up a triangle of toast, eyeing her with the patience of a true believer.

"It's an ancient craft. Intuition. Sensitivity. A quick grasp of the client's real desires. Nothing to it."

"Scares me a bit," Sylvie admitted.

"Why don't you drop round to my place and I'll give you a reading? On the house, eh?"

Sylvie cleared the plates and stacked the dishwasher.

"Great. Trouble is I'm hardly let off the leash at work just now – rehearsals. But soon, really soon, I'd love to, Kev." She sat down and poured a second mug of coffee, touching his hand in what she hoped would not be construed a condescending gesture. "Actually, I'm thinking of getting a car. It'll save time and, frankly, dragging back here from Barons Court late at night gives me the creeps. The other guys from the Rep go on to a club afterwards but I need my sleep. Must be getting old," she said, her laughter tinny as a cracked bell.

"My mate in Lambeth rents out cars. Good bloke. Runs a repair shop just off The Walk. Here, I'll write down his address. He won't rob you."

Kevin scribbled on one of Leslie's paper serviettes and leaned across the table, his robe gaping as he shoved it under her plate.

"Thanks. You're a pal. Look, don't take this the wrong way, Kevin, but what," she said, pointing, "happened to the bosom?"

He grinned, grabbing the loose folds of the candlewick to his manly chest. "Yeah, best polystyrene boobs in the business. From the States. Brilliant, aren't they? I need them for my drag act."

"You work clubs?"

"Why not?"

"Because you're not really a transvestite, are you?" she

said gently, powered by a natural accord which had grown up between them over the scrambled eggs.

"It pays the bills."

Sylvie rose to go, an idea springing to mind. "Look here, why don't we give Leslie's fry-up a miss tonight? Are you free?"

She squeezed his arm, Big Sister all of a sudden, honestly warming to this clear-eyed guy who looked as if he had been dipping into the dressing-up box. "I'll level with you," she said, sensing his withdrawal. "I need a walker. You know what I mean? I'm a lone female, a stranger in this town. I must dig out some stuff about my sister who died in strange circumstances. That's why I'm here. It may turn out to be dangerous – I'm not sure what I'm getting myself into. Will you help me out?"

"Leslie said your sister may have killed herself?"

Sylvie paced the room, lighting a cigarette, her hair veiled in smoke. "Possibly. But Adele was all the family I had left apart from my mother in Canada who is entirely taken up with her new husband. I loved my sister. I can't let it go."

"Let me give you a tarot reading."

She turned on him impatiently. "I need more than a bloody voice from the grave, Kevin. Won't you help me?"

"Dinner?"

"Dinner. There's this restaurant. Le Pendu. I have to check it out. Will you come with me? Watch my back?"

"Where is this place?"

"Somewhere near Waterloo. D'you know it?"

He shook his head.

"Well, what do you say? My treat. I'll buy you dinner and you give me a free reading. Quits?"

He nodded. "I'll tell Leslie he'll have to cook on his own tonight, shall I? I'm not booked at the club Wednesdays."

She kissed him on both cheeks, grinning like a fool,

suddenly feeling things were finally looking up. He pushed her away, looking worried.

"What shall I wear?"

Sylvie burst into a paroxysm of giggles, hugging herself in helpless mirth.

"Isn't that my line?" she said at last.

"I do do straight," he assured her, "and the nails are optional."

"What about the turban?"

He whipped it off revealing a skull as bald as an egg.

"It was the radiotherapy," he whispered. "I had this tumour, see. It's OK now. But my hair never grew properly after so I just shave off what's left."

Sylvie's heart lurched. "Oh, Kevin, you poor darling." She rallied after a moment. "Well, I think you look dandy just as you are. I'll pick you up at eight, shall I? Call in for you at the magic shop? I hope to have some transport by then but, if not, we'll take a taxi."

He fished out his card from a stack of bills and correspondence behind the kitchen clock and said, "What did you say this place at Waterloo's called?"

"Le Pendu. Terrible name for an eatery. Spooky."

"Le Pendu?"

"The Hanged Man. The bloke who owned it was murdered a couple of nights ago but it's still open for business. I checked."

"The Hanged Man," Kevin murmured. "Poor devil must have had a premonition."

Ian Preston had taken to ringing Sylvie after midnight which in any normal household would have caused ructions, the telephone shrilling in the sparsely carpeted landing like a fire alarm. But Leslie's boarders, embroiled in their post-performance rake-overs and heated commentary on his late night viewing choices, carried on their own racket in the communal living room unperturbed by their lengthy confabs and Sylvie's carrying voice.

Despite her initial reservations, Sylvie found herself attracted to this Odd Man Out. A complex bloke and far from her usual type, his buttoned-up attitudes only melting in the warmth of her response. Shivering in the chilly hallway, sharing the sheer bloody turmoil of their current workload, Sylvie found the empathy of a virtual stranger a solace over-riding her reluctance to get into a relationship when sorrow had already stripped layers from her emotional defences.

Adele was dead. Her only sister. Her friend and confidante. Originally torn apart all those years ago at that traumatic period in their lives when their parents had split, Sylvie had spent half her life in Canada and Adele had carved a place for herself in England. Both had suffered. Despite the difference in their ages and despite the thousands of miles put between them, the blood tie was unbreakable, Adele's persistence in maintaining the contact spanning the break and her step-mother's prohibition had, if anything, cemented the bond.

As women they had met as often as Sylvie's stagework allowed, and she had grown up sure in the knowledge that Adele loved her as she had loved no-one else. If Adele had married happily, found the right man, had children, this affinity between them may have been diluted, but sharing a history of poor relationships the two became emotionally indivisible.

But Sylvie's heartfelt belief that she had known Adele through and through was damaged. Since the drowning, realisation was dawning that Adele was, in fact, a mystery. Had she, in fact, known her at all?

Ian Preston had come into her life as Adele had left it. One door opens as another closes: wasn't that what her mother had so often repeated in her broken English which those years living in Cambridge had never eradicated?

Their late-night musings spilled over into snatched moments when Sylvie rang him on his mobile phone but they needed to be together: whispered confidences during his working day merely fanned the frustration. Their weekend together could not come soon enough it seemed for either of them, both secretly uncertain of this wave of mutual need which had inexplicably struck like a spring tide but neither brave enough to question the irrational attraction.

Finally, after a tearful outburst following a particularly painful reappraisal of Adele's possible suicide, Sylvie asked Ian to cancel the two rooms booked in Cambridge over the weekend.

"What! You mean it?" he spluttered.

Her voice grew calmer. "Yes. I'm sure. Make it a double room. I need your arms around me, honey, even if it's only for the one night. What do you say?"

Sixteen

When Sylvie drew up and tooted her horn outside Kevin's magic shop, his face appeared at the lighted window upstairs and she stepped on to the pavement to give him a wave.

The place was closed but the shop window remained illuminated and the suspended crystals twinkled as they revolved under concealed lighting shafting down eerily from behind a frilly pelmet. Candles, japanese masks and books on auras, colour therapy and DIY exorcism were displayed against a backdrop of black velvet embroidered with stars. In a corner of the window Kevin's card had been blown-up and given a spotlight all of its own. It read:

> Visions by Vanda,
> Astrology, Tarot & Palm Readings.
> No appointment necessary.
> Hours: 2–5 pm.

Sylvie was still studying the window as the door silently opened and for a moment she was unaware of this slight interruption to her fascination with the shop – the like of which, commonplace in New York where such psychic advice centres were as acceptable as psychiatrists' offices, was an unexpected find in a part of London where sex shops and massage parlours paid dearly for the prime location.

It was only when the man a few yards from her started locking up the shop door, activating several locks and obsessively checking the security that Sylvie realised that her companion for the evening did, in fact, "do straight" as he said at breakfast.

"Hey, Kevin! You look really cute."

He grinned. "Yeah, well the nails took a bit of shifting but if I was to be your walker I thought I'd let the hairy bits get an airing."

He wore jeans and a beige polo shirt and moccasins polished like chestnuts, topped off with a fogeyish tweed jacket which smelt of joss sticks.

"You didn't recognise me at first did you?" he quipped. "It's the hair. D'you like it?"

"It's fabulous." And indeed it was. The brownish wig was obviously top-grade and featured a smooth ponytail secured by an elastic band, the whole effect entirely natural and utterly convincing. She affectionately squeezed his arm and dropped an A–Z street guide into his lap as they settled in the car.

"Nice motor."

"I got it from your friend, Tony. Showed him your card and hey presto – wheels!" The car was a small two-door saloon, neatly vacuumed and exhibiting a strident notice banning smoking.

"You'll have to navigate, Kevin, I'll need all my wits about me just getting myself in the right lane." He proved an excellent guide and, in no time, they had spotted Le Pendu and found a parking space nearby.

The restaurant occupied a corner site in a side street tucked away behind the National Theatre. The diners were partly hidden by cafe curtains but the place was clearly limping along and Sylvie realised that booking ahead from the rehearsal rooms after Ian Preston had given her a buzz could hardly have been less necessary. Ian sounded pretty depressed, the visiting inspector having entirely unpicked the Morrison investigation without, so far, having discovered anything new.

"She hasn't caught up with Underwood yet?"

"Not so far. Threatens to drag me down to London with her to flush him out. God knows whose budget this re-hash will crucify. My super's doing his nut already."

"What's his place called?"

"Whose place?"

"Underwood's. You said he had a shop."

"I said he had a place *over* a shop. Trade Winds. Why do you ask?"

"Idle curiosity. I can't believe that the entire police force can't track down one missing witness. Lack of resources don't they call it?" she joked, feeling his mood lightening as a burgeoning warmth softened the bleakness of their current career frustrations. She outlined her disastrous interview with the producer that morning when presenting herself as the spokesperson for the moaning coterie who forecast the doom not only of the show but of the reputation of Garnett's Rep – in a business chock-a-block with new talent pushing from behind like a herd of wildebeest. She said nothing about her date that night with Kevin Last. She needed no crystal ball to guess that insinuating herself into Ferguson's restaurant would not go down well with her very own detective inspector.

"Did you get yourself a mobile?"

"Not yet."

"Bloody hell, Sylvie, what are you playing at? Life's difficult enough."

"Look, I've got to go. I'll be in touch. OK for Friday night?" she added with that breathy delivery audiences had learned to know and love.

He melted on cue. "Yes, sure. I've got us a room at the Old Spotted Cow on the Granchester road. I'll meet you there, shall I? As soon as you can make it, angel.

I've booked us in for dinner and there's a raincheck on Saturday night as well if we can swing it. I'm hoping that harpy Wilkinson will have flown back to the big city by the weekend."

She hurried back to the rehearsal stage, seemingly oblivious to the razor edge of the director's glance as she slid on to her chalk mark and stepped into Mrs Elvsted's shoes once again.

The solitary waiter at Le Pendu greeted them effusively, taking Sylvie's raincoat and ushering them to a table near the bar. The lighting was subdued but welcoming, the napery crisp and the other diners, mostly young, seemed to be having a good time.

"A drink, Kevin?"

"Wine?"

"I don't know much about wine. You choose," she said, passing over the wine list and concentrating on the menu. Asking Kevin along had been a wise move, dropping in here unescorted might have been uncomfortable in such a sparsely occupied dining room though the waiter was affable enough and the dress code of the other diners slick but unthreateningly smart. Sylvie had had no chance to change after rehearsal but her ankle-length black skirt and pink linen top seemed acceptable and the interested glances which settled on their table were not, Kevin reassured himself, drawn by his wig.

They respectively chose garlic mushrooms and pâté as starters, dipping from each other's plates and murmuring appreciatively when the red snapper and calves' liver took over.

Kevin ate sparingly but with an attention to detail which Sylvie, normally unimpressed by foodie talk, found both illuminating and fair.

They dawdled over dessert and coffee, Sylvie lighting up with alacrity while Kevin, still mesmerised by the menu, scrutinised the delicacies they had missed out on.

"Great chef. Underpriced though."

"Has a whiff of desperation about the place if you ask me," she whispered. "Could start by losing the name."

"The Hanged Man? Perhaps it was called that before. It's unlucky to change the name of a house, probably the same for restaurants."

Their fellow diners and the waiter had all slipped away before Sylvie called for the bill and the chef himself emerged from below bearing the folded bill on a plate. The man had the prison pallor of a kitchen slave but a nice smile and wafted a warm aroma of olive oil with his goodbye wave to the mousy girl who handled the accounts and took the telephone bookings.

"Terrific menu," Kevin enthused, his genuine appreciation giving the chef's exhaustion a lift.

"Won't you join us for a nightcap?" Sylvie suggested. "No more customers tonight, even your waiter's pushed off home."

He smiled and without a word went to the bar, returning with three brandy glasses and a bottle of cognac on a tin tray. He introduced himself as Terry Barker, shaking hands all round and, at Kevin's prompting, launched into a mini cv beginning with his lowly status as sous chef at a prestigious restaurant, the mere mention of which caused Kevin's eyes to glaze with wonder. The name meant nothing to Sylvie and, taking a deep breath, she said with all the nonchalance of a real trouper, "The owner here was James Ferguson, wasn't he? The bloke who got drowned in that mindless attack on the bridge. It was all over the papers."

"The police should keep someone permanently on duty on that bloody footbridge," Terry exploded, his red-rimmed eyes sparking with emotion. "Never should have happened. Low life of every sort there all the bleeding hours of the day and night, pimping, begging, ganging up on people like Jimmy stupid enough to be there in the small hours. Asking for trouble!"

"Terrible thing. Has it knocked your bookings?"

"Wednesdays are always a bit thin, specially at the end of the month before people get paid. We worked it up together, Jimmy and me. The place is all mine now, God help me – we had this legal agreement. If either of us died his share passed to the survivor. Saved a lot of messing with his ex-wife or my greedy relatives. It was a good partnership though. He played front of house and I did what I like best. But that's all over now."

"You're giving up?"

"No choice. Unless the bank gives me a breather. I can't swing it alone. Jimmy was in the process of buttering up a new backer when he died."

"Won't this backer put up for *you*? The chef's the key in a place like this," Kevin blurted out. "Front men are easily replaced."

"But we were pals, it wasn't just a business for Jimmy – it was his life."

Undeterred, Kevin blundered on. "How much would it take for you to soldier on here? It's a great opportunity what with all the redevelopment along the river."

The chef sipped his firewater, fixing on Kevin with the melancholy gaze of a spaniel in quarantine.

"Only a lousy fifty grand," he said. "But you know what bankers are like."

"This new backer your partner was negotiating with – another restaurateur wanting to expand?"

"Never met him myself. Jimmy was introduced to him at a wine tasting. Our supplier knew this bloke Toomey, knew we were having to update our equipment and suggested they had a drink together. I rang him on his mobile after the murder but he's lost the taste for it he says. Thinks Le Pendu's got a jinx. Probably right."

"Would you show me round?" Kevin put in, clearly all fired up by the chef's tale of woe.

Terry Barker's eyes hardened. "You're not a pair of them incognito restaurant critics, are you?"

"I'm an actress," Sylvie swiftly put in, "but this young man has a natural feeling for places. Senses the vibes."

"It's not got a bad aura," Kevin said in all seriousness, "but you'll have to take a chance and change the name."

"Yeah, not a bad idea. Always wondered about it myself. But Le Pendu was Jimmy's idea. The Hanged Man. As it happens only one punter in a hundred knows what Le Pendu means so I don't reckon what name we call it makes a fat lot of difference. Anyway, come and see the kitchen, folks. I've got a smashing pair of galley slaves down there, two Spanish lads, would work their balls off to keep this place open."

Sylvie excused herself from the cook's tour and lit another cigarette, mulling over the curious road she had taken on this hopeless quest for something, anything, that would explain away her doubts about Adele's death. Maybe Kevin was right. Maybe a voice from the grave *was* what she was hankering after.

Terry Barker and her date for the evening spent over half an hour touring the premises and when they re-emerged to lock up they found Sylvie fast asleep, her head on her arms on the table, cigarette butts overflowing the ashtray.

On the way home Kevin remained silent, perking up only when they reached the boarding house, coming to with a start to thank Sylvie effusively for "a marvellous evening".

She eyed him doubtfully as she locked the car. "It wasn't that terrific, boyo. You don't have to lay it on with a trowel."

He stopped her at the kerb, searching for a sign of assurance.

"Look, I've been thinking about what you said. You're right. I'm not really into this cross-dressing lark. It was a joke at first, something to hide behind when I lost my hair. But I've got to get out. Now. Before it's too late. Leslie's been good to me but I think I've got a chance here."

"Terry offered you a job at Le Pendu?"

"Jimmy's share."

"A partnership?" she gasped.

"Don't tell the others for Christ's sake. Truth is I've got a bit of a nest egg tucked away. My Gran left me her house in Birmingham. I've been letting it for years. If Terry can put off the bank manager while I sell it, I can put enough capital into it to put the place back on the road. It's got terrific potential."

"And Terry's willing to stick it out in the kitchen?"

"He *loves* cooking. The bloke's an artist," he enthused. "You can spot a winner a mile off."

"It wasn't a winner for James Ferguson. Quite the reverse."

"He was a marked man. Terry never knew why but it was obvious the guy was doomed."

"You're not serious? Doomed? You don't really believe all that doom stuff, do you, Kevin?" she said, shaking off his hand and waiting under the porch for Kevin to insert his key. "Anyway," she added, "if James and Terry were pals like he said, how come Terry didn't know what this 'doom' was that was hanging over him? Sounds fishy to me."

He stood his ground, his eyes burning. "Believe me or not, Sylvie, but I saw this coming."

"In your stars?" she chortled.

"If you like. Anyway, take my word for it, you only get one big chance in life and it's the opportunity you turn down that will haunt you. I've been hiding under that bloody turban too long."

She sobered, gripping his sleeve. "Listen to me, Kevin.

117

You know nothing about this restaurant guy. He could have cheated James Ferguson for years for all you know – could have been the mystery man who tipped him in the river! Thought of that? You could lose every penny you own, throw it into a money pit and find yourself back on the drag queen circuit. Sorry to be so negative but I'm older than you in years and tears."

"How old do you think I am, Sylvie?"

She shrugged. "Twenty? Twenty-two?"

"I'll be thirty years old next month."

"Jeepers! You should forget the catering business and invest in a wrinkle cream factory. You could clean up, believe me."

"I'm serious."

She sighed. "Yes, I know you are. And I'm sorry to joke about it, but please promise me one thing. Don't sign *anything* until you've had the books checked by a reputable accountant. A deal?"

He grinned, turning the key in the lock, the roar from Leslie's gang watching the big match on the telly erupting from the living room like a Cup Final action replay.

Kevin scuttled up the stairs to change, unwilling to face the barrage of questions that "doing straight" would emanate from the boarders, leaving Sylvie to join them for a last cigarette. Leslie shoved up on the sofa and made a space for her, his lips pursed in a silent kiss. They whispered like kids in the back row, their words buried in the fallout from the telly.

"Been out on the town with my Kevin I hear. Naughty, naughty. Girly talk?"

"I took him to a place to have his palm read."

"*His* palm?"

"Sure. Why not? You didn't know I had a magic circle of my own did you, Leslie?"

She hauled herself from the low couch and, miming fond

farewells to the soccer fans rivetted by extra time, bent down to whisper in Leslie's ear.

"I introduced him to a hanged man and he showed your Kevin a way to make his turban disappear."

Seventeen

Rehearsals seemed to shake down quite nicely once Rennie Coles got over the sulks and the general consensus of the Rep's old guard was that Harry Garnett had bribed his new director with lunch at The Ivy, a cure-all for theatricalities in Harry's book.

Sylvie's preoccupation with Adele's last days immured her from the cast's passions over this particular production and Harry's unexpected offer of the weekend off, including Friday afternoon, was greeted with unanimous relief.

Harry Garnett was a cunning operator but such a diplomatic gesture as a free afternoon when the old stagers were all too well aware that the performance was still way off, invited ribald speculation on the producer's warming relationship with the new leading lady. It looked as if Joanna was likely to prove the next recipient of the aging Garnett's attentions, the long weekend likely shrouded under the mantle of "personal rehearsals" for the demanding Hedda role. Sylvie was amused by the man's covert advances, her own dalliance with the boss having long run out of steam. Since she herself no longer commanded such one-to-one "coaching", she found herself newly embraced within the Garnett clique, the diminution of unspoken jealousies making her suddenly popular.

Straight after lunch she packed an overnight bag and popped in to say cheerio to Leslie, having had no chance to speak to Kevin since their dinner date on Wednesday night.

"Where's Kevin?"

"Gone up north to see to some family business," Leslie confided, tapping his nose in comical overemphasis. "He's got money of his own, you know. Makes a packet out of that Madame Arcarti lark, the fortune telling scams. It don't stop at just a reading you know, Sylv. Before the poor bloody punter gets out the door Kevin's sold her a bunch of them dangly glass things to hang in her window, books, lucky charms, you name it. Gets a rake off from the woman what owns the shop shouldn't wonder."

"Has Kevin done your chart yet, Leslie?"

"Not bloody likely! Won't even tell him my star sign in case he runs off a forecast on his computer on the quiet. Wouldn't put it past him."

"On his *computer?*"

"Regular customers ring up and he sends by return, all typed up like a bleeding balance sheet. Can't say the boy ain't a grafter but for meself I don't like tempting fate, messing with all that astrology shit."

"You don't believe in it?"

"Too right I don't. Not that I ain't superstitious. Us in the entertainment business, Sylvie, don't invite bad luck, do we, gel?" He rapped playfully against her temple. "Knock on wood, I say."

"Look, I'm going to Cambridge for the weekend, Leslie. If anyone rings I'll be back Sunday night. OK?"

She manoeuvred out of a tight parking spot outside the boarding house, treating the little hire car with serious respect, her own tight budget leaving little leeway for unnecessary expenses and far from certain whether shacking up with Ian Preston at the Old Spotted Cow was wise after such a short acquaintance.

Would he expect her to go Dutch? she gloomily reflected. You're getting quite morbid these days, Sylvie Reynolds. A nice weekend in the country is probably just what the doctor ordered.

The day was unseasonably hot, the September sun bathing the city streets in a warm glow. Having plenty of time to spare before Fiona expected her for a drink after work in the wine bar opposite the solicitors' office, Sylvie drove across town for a second look at Le Pendu, reassured by the clutch of people enjoying lunch at tables set outside under a striped awning, the garlicky aroma wafting through her lowered window as she kerb crawled past setting her taste buds on edge. She decided to pick up a sandwich before joining the motorway but found herself doubling back towards the common. Quite the wrong direction.

In her heart she admitted she had had this little detour in mind from the very first moment Harry Garnett provided this window of opportunity. Kevin would say it was Fate but really it amounted to nothing more than blind determination. The urge to speak with Adele's last Romeo, the elusive Brendon Underwood, was too hard to resist. She had already looked up Trade Winds in the telephone directory and pulled to the side of the road to check her A–Z.

Hardly off route at all, she lied to herself, her desire to put a face to the final name on Adele's roll call of admirers pulling her through the maze of back streets like a fish on a line.

Trade Winds was a travel agency operating just off Lavender Hill. The place looked prosperous, invitingly garish posters promising glorious winter breaks and cut-price cruises filled the window. Inside, soft calypso music set the tone and the two girls manning the desk were beautifully tanned, themselves terrific ads for the good life.

The dark one looked up from a stack of brochures as Sylvie walked in, a tuneful jangle from the bell above the door cheerful as birdsong.

"Hi! Just browsing or would you like some of these?" she said with a grin, holding up a sheaf of rainbow offers hot off the press.

"Actually, I'm looking for Mr Underwood."

"Brendon's office is upstairs. It's your lucky day, he's just dropped in. Always on the move that guy – our best customer." She pointed to a spiral staircase snaking up behind the counter. Sylvie smiled nervously, edging to the stairs, wondering if, as on Wednesday night, it would have been sensible to drag Kevin along. But that was stupid. What was she afraid of? At worst the man would tell her to bugger off and mind her own business.

She climbed the iron staircase and knocked on a door off the landing where a brass plate announced Underwood Books. By Appointment Only.

A deep voice with a faintly Irish inflection issued from behind the door. "That you, Victoria? Coffee already?" Sylvie's mouth was as dry as dust and the words just would not come. "Hold on a tick," he shouted.

The door swung open and Sylvie found herself confronted with Adele's client-cum-lover, Brendon Underwood. The man looked puzzled but smiled encouragingly.

"Hey, sorry. Thought it was one of the girls from downstairs. They top up my caffeine intake when I blow in."

Sylvie held out her hand, beaming foolishly, and found her voice at last.

"My name's Reynolds. Sylvie . . . I was just passing and thought I'd d-drop in to see you," she stuttered. "I hope you don't mind. My sister was Adele Morrison," she added.

His smile faded but he ushered her in, confused it would seem by the unscheduled appearance of a girl he could hardly credit to be blood-related to the fair, sylphlike Adele, except there was something . . . A snapshot in Adele's cottage? Two dark-haired women outside a cafe, drinking wine.

"Please forgive me. Come in. Excuse my staring – Adele's sister you say. She often spoke of you. Here, let me open the window. It's so warm in here, been shut up for a couple of weeks. I've been abroad you

123

see – on a buying trip . . ." His voice finally petered out, this burbling welcome barely masking his genuine astonishment. "I thought you were in Canada."

Sylvie nodded, remaining tongue-tied, her mixed-up emotions jumbling the preconceptions of this man which she had built up in her mind. She found herself drawn into an office stacked from floor to ceiling with volumes, the musty smell of old print and yellowing pages stifling in that enclosed space.

Underwood had clearly just arrived, his briefcase tossed on the desk, his jacket draped over the back of the chair. He wore a striped shirt and a snazzy silk tie reeking of Paris, his grey hair tousled, his face now cleanshaven. Sylvie trained to sum up a character in moments was caught on her back foot by his unforeseen charm, his smile sweet as a nut, his eyes wrinkled from years and years on the road. A sort of super salesman.

"Look here, Sylvie. May I call you Sylvie? This place is airless. Let's go out for tea, shall we? There's a wonderful bread shop just up the road that has a few tables at the back. Superb muffins. Would that be OK?"

Eighteen

When she arrived at the rendezvous Fiona was already up at the bar talking to a man who looked vaguely familiar.

"Hey, Sylvie! I'd almost given you up."

"Sorry. Traffic's terrible. Everyone in London is making a break for it while this Indian summer holds."

"You remember Gary, don't you? From the – er – memorial for Adele. Another estate agent I'm afraid."

Sylvie smiled and shook hands with Fiona's sidekick, a Gallic gesture which very nearly dented his aplomb but he rallied superbly, mouthing sympathetic noises about her late sister.

"You almost said 'party' didn't you Fiona? Actually I don't mind if you call it a party. Adele would have found a cheerful wake eminently appropriate. It was awfully good of you, Fiona, rallying all her friends for a decent send-off like that."

She pecked Fiona's cheek, squeezing her arm in greeting.

"Well, *you* didn't hang about, decent send-off or not."

Sylvie demurred, unwilling, in the company of this avid mate of Fiona's to launch into an explanation of her need to drag Ian Preston back to Suffolk to get the real lowdown on the inquest.

"You'll have to excuse me, ladies, I've got a date."

Fiona made a grimace. "And all this time I thought it was me you were chatting up for the night's entertainment, Gary."

"Next waltz with me. OK? I'll ring you, Fiona," he said, sketching a farewell to his other buddies before slipping off into the dusk.

"Seems a nice bloke," Sylvie remarked.

"Got a lovely house in the city too. Trouble with Cambridge is it's stuffed with gorgeous talent, new girls arriving by the boatload every October – gives us residents one hell of a lot of competition."

Fiona leaned across the bar, giving the barman her Medusa look which resulted in her jumping the queue in moments.

"I've ordered a bottle of Chablis. He'll bring it over, just grab a table will you while I pop to the penny house."

Fiona bustled off through the crowd, her dark-suited figure carving a path through the Friday night crowd like the parting of the Red Sea. Sylvie nabbed a corner table and the waiter tailed her with a bottle in an ice bucket.

The place was untrammelled by students, the Michaelmas term yet to chug into gear and, as Sylvie waited for Fiona to reappear, she found herself contemplating a room full of seriously suited young men and long-legged girls in designer gear. Presumably, once the youngsters moved in the professional crowd would move on. Or perhaps the students stuck to their own territory, giving the salaried clique a wide berth. "The gold fillings of society" sprung to mind, an all-embracing phrase which cut out strolling players like herself and certainly excluded policemen such as Ian Preston.

Sylvie signalled Fiona from across the room and she pushed her way through to join her. She had taken to Fiona from the word "go" – the woman's generous assessment of Adele's complicated life in no way spoiling their relationship. Fiona had enfolded Sylvie into her own circle and was, it had to be admitted, the nearest she could claim in her present circumstances to a Best Friend.

126

They filled in the blanks since the party, Sylvie admitting to her growing closeness to Ian Preston.

"The whole business has broken out again I hear," Fiona remarked, "since Adele's old flame got murdered."

"James Ferguson. Yes. I'm hoping Ian will have news when I see him tonight. They've sent another inspector to check out Adele's involvement with Ferguson. It's only the question of the hotel key found in his pocket that links them still. Weird thing that."

"I read about it in the papers. Do you think she was still stringing him along after all these years?"

Sylvie shrugged. "Who knows? The more I learn about my darling sister, the more I realise we hardly knew her at all."

Fiona poured the wine, her face troubled.

"There's a simple explanation to the key business, you'll see. And if she was still seeing him, so what? He had a nice restaurant business in London it seems. Never remarried, no possible reason why he and Adele shouldn't get together again. Perhaps he thought she might have mellowed, would feel more vulnerable to his renewed advances," she added with a lift of the eyebrow.

"His restaurant wasn't a gold mine, Fiona. He was looking for another backer just to bail them out. It was a joint venture, the chef is trying to get it back on the road."

"Trouble is any sort of bistro in central London has to fight off competition like crazy just to keep afloat. Even fashionable places go off the boil for no reason at all and poof," she said, throwing both hands in the air.

"You would know, Fifi."

"Fifi! Did Adele tell you she called me that? Brings tears to my eyes, your voices are so similar."

"Sure she did. Fifi. It suits you. Blows away that legal-eagle look you've acquired since we first knew each other."

"You may mock but I know what I'm talking about. But,

getting back to what I was saying, clients of mine have got their fingers burnt backing restaurants. Some have even gone bankrupt."

"I can believe it. I'm worried about a friend of mine who's thinking of buying into the partnership at Le Pendu, the Ferguson place."

"The Hanged Man?"

"You know it?"

"No. But my French isn't that rusty, you condescending cow. What else have you been up to?"

"Rehearsals mostly. You must come and see the new production next month. I'll send some tickets. It's 'Hedda Gabler'."

"Grief! No thanks. Ibsen makes me want to rush out of the theatre and lay down in the road. I'll pass on that one, sweetie. And I thought actresses led such interesting lives. Silly old me."

Sylvie leaned across the table. "If you promise to keep your mouth shut, I'll tell you something really interesting."

Fiona perked up, refilling their glasses, forgetting even to object when Sylvie lit up a cigarello, wreathing their heads in pungent smoke.

"I went to see Underwood."

"What!"

Sylvie nodded. "Adele's last date. I just had to come to some sort of conclusion. To ask him what really happened that night."

"And?"

"Nothing we didn't know already. Adele got pushy as always, they had a row and he walked out. But he's a really nice guy, Fiona, he really opened up."

"Underwood's a shit. Promised to marry Adele and then lied about it."

"Did you know his wife died?"

"I thought he wasn't married."

"He isn't. But he was. She died six years ago. Hanged herself from the bannisters while he was away on a trip."

"Jesus! I'm sure Adele knew nothing about that, she would have told me. Why would he confide in you? Have you been meeting him in London? What on earth does Ian think about this?"

"Ian musn't know. I only met Brendon once but we had a long talk. He told me everything. I cried."

"You cried?"

"Yes. It was so tragic. Fancy getting an e-mail to tell you your wife's killed herself?"

Fiona choked back a sharp riposte, knowing Sylvie to be deeply sympathetic to the man who was obviously playing on her emotions, and tried to bring some logic into play.

"It never came out at the inquest this business about his wife's suicide. If he had been more forthcoming it might have bolstered the suggestion the pool attendant made that Adele drowned herself deliberately. Total rubbish, of course. All her friends know Adele wasn't the sort to top herself. She got depressed. We all do at times. But she was a survivor. Underwood clearing out would have been a temporary upset as far as your sister was concerned."

"That's what he said."

"At least you've got something clear. You half thought she might have killed herself, didn't you, Sylvie? What else did he say?"

"Apparently his wife was hopeless on her own and he travelled abroad a lot. The neighbours found her. He never speaks of it as a rule but he wanted to reassure me about Adele. Put my mind at rest. He didn't want me to be burdened for the rest of my life with the conviction that she had planned to die. Brendon's had to live with that himself for the past six years, the guilt scars you for life even when it's not remotely any fault of your own."

"Bully for him."

"Why do you hate him so much?"

"Just a feeling. Call it envy if you like. Adele always played the field – and I can't even get that wanker Gary into my bed," she added with a bitter laugh.

Sylvie slapped Fiona's hand as it lay on the table and continued with her story. She really was busting to share this secret meeting with Brendon with someone and it was all too evident that Ian would take her tête-à-tête as a serious interference in this reopened investigation.

"And you believe this guy Underwood?"

"No-one could lie so convincingly. He was trembling, actually trembling just speaking about it."

"Why you? He'd never even seen you before."

"I begged him to tell me what happened and telling me about his wife's suicide explained why he didn't hang around after the inquest, didn't feel he owed anyone any explanations about Adele's state of mind the night she died. Then I came along. I'd flown from Canada specially. She was my only sister. I loved her, Fiona, and he recognised my need to be comforted. Yes, I did think it wasn't an accident, not necessarily suicide but it was a possibility I couldn't ignore. He answered all my questions and now I'm satisfied. Adele was drunk and she died in a stupid accident. Nobody's fault. Simple as that."

Fiona leaned back, assessing Sylvie's pain. No doubt about it whatever sort of liar one might rate Underwood, he had set Sylvie free to get on with the rest of her life. Why knock it?

Sylvie rushed on, the words bubbling up like champagne from a shaken bottle. "He's been living out of a suitcase since his wife died. Hotels. Villas abroad. Couldn't bring himself to make a new home for himself. Then Adele came along and at first he was really in love with her. But you know Adele, Fiona, probably better than anyone. She persuaded him that what he really needed was a big country house so they could both work from home."

"He's some sort of dealer isn't he?"

"Antique maps and books. It was his late father-in-law's firm apparently. His wife had a substantial private income, the book business was merely a sort of family hobby but Brendon got interested and sticks at it for lack of anything else to take his mind off the tragedy."

"He's that rich?"

Sylvie nodded.

"And still unmarried? Can't you introduce me to this chap? Suddenly all my reservations about Mr Underhand Underwood have melted away," she said with a grin.

Sylvie glanced at her watch. "Look, sorry it's been such a rush, Fifi, but I'll look in on Sunday afternoon, shall I? To pick up the rest of my gear? You can ring me at the Old Spotted Cow if something nicer hovers on to the horizon after Sunday lunch."

They left in a rush, Fiona to change before a cinema date with her trainee, a sweet natured black girl new in town, and Sylvie to find her way to the Granchester road.

Her evening with Ian was less than wonderful, he being seriously unrelaxed, excusing himself twice in the course of dinner to take phone calls.

Sylvie was toying with her crêpe Suzette when he returned from this second call and said, "Look here, Ian. Shall we call it a day? You've obviously had second thoughts about this. No hard feelings but I'd feel more comfortable if we cleared the air."

He took her hand in both of his and made a fervent appeal, practically on his knees all of a sudden.

"I can't tell you how bad I feel about this, darling, but I've got to drive to London first thing tomorrow. Can't we go together? I'll explain the details in the morning – we mustn't spoil our one night together, must we?"

"What's up?"

He took a deep breath. "They've had Morrison in for questioning all afternoon. He's agreed to go on a line-up."

"A line-up?"

"One of the lads who witnessed the attack on Ferguson thinks he would recognise the killer. He wore a striped scarf he said, described it pretty accurately."

"A football scarf?"

"Sounds like it. But the fact remains Morrison could fit this bloke's description and when they took him in he produced a ticket stub from his wallet for a Festival Hall concert that evening. Admits he was there that night."

"Cunning sod. He must have guessed it would probably come out."

"He denies being there so late, of course he does. And as soon as this witness passes him up on the identity parade they'll let him go."

"But the witnesses were all drunk. They said so at the time. Why set off on this tack?"

"They can't just dismiss Morrison out of hand. There's other circumstantial evidence. I don't know all of it but at least they're letting me sit in on the investigation."

"You don't think he did it, do you, Ian?"

"Takes strength to chuck a man off a bridge. But Morrison kept himself pretty fit. Looks like a bag of bones but does cross-country running apparently. God knows how he does it: I got the impression he was practically a chain smoker but he says he only took up smoking again after his wife died. The shock . . ."

"Adele? He called Adele his wife?"

"Always refers to her as his wife. Makes no excuse about hating Ferguson for breaking up his marriage and according to my new running mate, the delectable Inspector Wilkinson, Morrison's phone bill lists dozens of calls to your sister – must have driven her crazy."

"What set all that off?"

"The nuisance calls?" Ian shrugged. "Search me. But at a guess I'd say he found out she was seeing Ferguson again. The man was still bitter about the way he had been chucked. Obsessive, I'd say, nothing much else to think about."

"After all these years?"

"The chef at Ferguson's place reckons he saw Morrison hanging about outside over the past month. He tackled Ferguson about it but he said it was some sad bastard he used to know from years ago. Said he'd deal with it. The chef's also agreed to attend this identity parade in the morning. I've got to go. Will you give me a second chance? I deserve it – the room's pretty good, and if you had tasted that expensive meal I set before you, you might agree that a re-run could only prove my point."

They passed on coffee, trailing through the smoky saloon bar to their room upstairs at the back of the pub, entwined in a desperate attempt to salvage what might have been a lovely weekend.

Nineteen

The Old Spotted Cow proved so agreeable and their night of bliss so unexpectedly relaxed that Sylvie decided to stay on over Saturday night. Having no desire to rush back to spend the weekend at the boarding house, a quiet day alone with her script was probably the best option.

Playing Elvsted had been a matter of convenience and her attention to the whole production disgracefully casual. Her attitude was not, as the rest of the cast surmised, a case of having her nose put out of joint in taking a minor role, but a selfish preoccupation with the Adele factor. Now that Underwood had put the demon Suicide back in its box, she admitted to a decent sense of guilt at the way in which she had walked through the scenes with Hedda, mouthing the all too familiar words, contributing the barest minimum to what was, in fact, a pivotal sequence of the drama.

Having a whole day to get to grips with the character at last fired new enthusiasm for the cameo role, the room above the saloon bar proving surprisingly accommodating to her belated concentration in the part she had wangled out of Garnett for herself.

Ian telephoned in the late afternoon, clearly exhausted by the questions raised by the Ferguson enquiry. It was as if Ferguson, his chef, Morrison and Adele had been performing an intricate dance of death, three members of this quadrille still entwined after years of bitterness, only the chef, Terry Barker, bringing fresh variations to the intricate steps.

"How did it go?" she asked.

"Pretty well despite Morrison's crackpot attitude. Anyone would think he *wanted* to be arrested. Even admitted to wearing a scarf – a college item as it happens, not the knitted football scarf the witness described, but striped in the same colours as our drunk said."

"But they let him go?"

"Bound to. The identity parade was a farce. Getting a line-up of blokes looking like Cambridge academics wasn't easy, especially on a weekend, but Wilkinson roped in a likely looking crew and, true to form, our only witness picked out a retired copper dragged in for a laugh."

"They're convinced Morrison's innocent?"

"Not exactly convinced but they had to let him go – not enough evidence."

"Did he explain his nuisance calls to Adele?"

"Sure. Said he always kept a close watch on his wife and any dubious men friends she encountered. Considered it his duty. Said he was protecting her."

"From Ferguson?"

"Yeah. Silly old sod's spent hours tracking down information about her boyfriends. Your sister was practically under surveillance. One thing was interesting. When Ferguson confronted him outside the restaurant and asked Morrison what his game was, Morrison accused him of having renewed his affair with your sister. Ferguson explained that he had only re-established contact with her after spotting Adele's website. Morrison admits he hit the roof, didn't like her advertising herself for all and sundry to gawp at. He specifically objected to 'my wife exhibiting herself like that' and it was this website thing which I suspect set him off on the flurry of nuisance calls. If Ferguson hadn't told him about it, Morrison would never have discovered it for himself – surfing the net not being his thing at all. He regarded the photograph as an incitement to perverts, he said, completely ignoring the fact that your sister was an astute businesswoman and that having a personal website is not tantamount to tacking up your card in a telephone box."

"He's completely batty. Has been for years, ever since Adele was named on Ferguson's divorce papers. You've seen this website?"

"Of course. It's perfectly OK. Purely commercial. Lists the services she offers as a property consultant and to my mind the photograph was pretty tasty too."

Sylvie lay back on the bed, gripping the receiver. "Can you get back here tonight, Ian?"

"No problem."

"Any other worms crawling out of the woodwork?"

"The chef, Barker, picked out Morrison, identified him as the man hanging about outside the restaurant on more than one occasion until Ferguson tackled him one night. He later told his partner what was on the bloke's mind. After being warned off, Morrison was assured by Jimmy Ferguson that his re-involvement with his wife was on a purely business footing but the chef reckoned Ferguson's stalker was unconvinced. Jealousy nurtured over a period of years only festers and Morrison admitted in the interview room that Ferguson's excuse that he was trying to interest Adele in putting money into Le Pendu was thin, and until the solicitor advised him of the inheritance that had fallen into his lap he was sceptical that his pretty wife had the ability to gather that much capital to refinance a restaurant. I don't have much time for the man but I genuinely got the impression he isn't interested in money – he probably thought Ferguson was putting him on, insisting Adele was merely a business contact."

"But Barker insists she was a serious investor, as well as his other backer, the man who withdrew after his partner died?"

"Ferguson was obviously a belt and braces man. Adele

had money to spare – pity you lost out on that hefty inheritance, Sylvie, Morrison didn't deserve to cop the lot and frankly I don't think he knows what to do with it, but I may be wrong."

"And Ferguson told the chef he was hoping to raise capital from Adele too?"

"A loan. A bundle of cash to tide things over until this backer bought his way into the business."

"Whew! Why was all the financial nous funnelled into one sister and not the other? I have trouble just keeping my credit cards in line," she added with a laugh.

"The chef said Ferguson was confident that Adele would bail them out till Toomey tipped up. 'An old friend' he told Barker but the loan would cost them a whole chunk in interest, she wasn't chipping in for free. They were really putting their shirts on this backer eventually coming up with the fifty grand."

"What next?"

"With the investigation you mean? We're at a dead end with the murder. Wilkinson's convinced herself it's more than a mugging but frankly she's got nothing to go on. Tanked-up drifters target single pedestrians fool enough to wander about after midnight in secluded blackspots like river walkways. Ferguson probably looked an easy touch and what started out as a robbery got out of hand when he fought back. Druggies get desperate and Ferguson was at the wrong place at the wrong time. Happens all over."

"Did the chef – Barker? – know why his partner was out on the streets so late that night?"

"Says Ferguson had a dinner date that evening. He had to pull in an extra waiter to stand in."

"Who with? His dinner date, I mean."

"The backer, Toomey. It was supposed to be a final meeting agreeing the terms of the new three-way partnership in Le Pendu. Ferguson met Toomey at the Savoy Grill – it's been confirmed, a reservation was made in

Toomey's name and he paid the bill. Quite a blow-out it seems. Ferguson must have been well-oiled if he shared all the booze charged on the chitty. Afterwards, Toomey – apparently he's a regular at the Savoy – got the doorman to call him a taxi, a big tipper by all accounts. And Ferguson walked off towards the Strand."

"Have you spoken to this backer?"

"No, but Wilkinson sent her sergeant to interview him though he's irrelevant to the investigation. But we did get excited when we found out he's got a record."

"For violence?"

"No, fraud. But he turned nasty in prison, an uncontrollable temper added years to his sentence. Changed his personality like it often does for the ones who've never been locked up before. In any case he's withdrawn from the deal, he said and, as he's kept his nose clean since he got out, there's no reason to harrass the poor sod. Anyway, I hear there's a new backer in the frame. A Kevin Last."

Sylvie sighed. "That was my fault."

"Didn't know you were chummy with rich investors. A personal friend of yours?" The question was bland enough but Sylvie wasn't fooled.

"You know bloody well Kevin lives at the same address as me. I'll have to explain when I see you tonight – it's too complicated to get into now. I tried to put him off but the boy's all fired up."

"Barker seems to think Last is a serious prospect. Do you know him well?"

"Well enough. For God's sake leave Kevin out of this Ferguson investigation, Ian. He's only come on the scene since the murder. Let's drop it, shall we? I'll book us in for dinner here tonight if you're sure you can make it. Eightish?"

"Make it nine."

In fact, he nearly didn't make it at all.

At eight-fifteen Sylvie answered the phone in her room,

all too ready for Ian's apologies, all too aware that dating a policeman played havoc with your social life.

"Hello, Sylvie? It's me, Fiona."

She relaxed. "Don't tell me. Something hunky's just walked in and our Sunday afternoon tea party's postponed."

"No, this is serious. Listen. I've had an anonymous letter pushed under my door."

"Dirty?"

"Worse. Totally unthreatening but reeking of menace, the words all blocked out in snippets cut from a newspaper like you see in the movies."

"Chuck it in the bin, Fifi. It's just one of your mates winding you up. God knows how you stick all those public schoolboy japes."

"No. It's about Adele. It says: 'Tell your friend, Sylvie, to put a bunch of heather on the grave of that kid Erica who was killed on the school trip in France. She'll find it in the churchyard of St Mary's at Bonningstone.'"

"What's that to do with Adele?"

"Adele and James Ferguson were the teachers in charge of a school holiday on which a child was killed. You never heard?"

Sylvie shook her head, warning bells clanging in horrible discord.

"You still there, Sylvie?"

"Yes, sorry. I'm all confused. What's this all about? And why dump this message on you?"

"Well, this nutty person must know we're close and, let's face it, you're not exactly in the phone book, are you, sweetie? Gives me the shivers, and I'm not the sort to quake at the knees with craziness like this. Perhaps someone heard you were back in England and wanted to put the boot in – underline Adele's nasty side just in case you hadn't heard. Didn't want her sister to have the delusion that she was an unspoilt virgin, eh? The child's mother was a total psycho I seem to remember from the newspaper reports – probably assumed you got Adele's money after she died. If you believed everything you saw in the papers you'd think Adele was absolutely loaded."

"I can't take all this in. You'll have to take me through it step by step. Oh, hang on, Ian's just walked through the door. You still OK for tomorrow afternoon? Right, we'll talk then. In the meantime please don't mention this to anyone – I've got to handle this in my own way. Promise?"

She put down the phone, her lip quivering as she hastily rose to hug the whey-faced stranger who looked as if he'd been on a treadmill all day.

"Who was that?" he said wearily.

"Oh, just the Stage Manager. Some sort of cock-up with rehearsals. I shall have to buzz off straight after lunch tomorrow, honey. Isn't it the pits? Seems as if this weekend's been blighted from the start."

He took her in his arms, nuzzling the musky scent of her hair, pushing her backwards on to the rumpled counterpane.

"Oh, I wouldn't say that."

Twenty

Sunday was Kevin's day off. Usually, after helping Leslie dish up the Sunday roast, a feast set out at the big kitchen table and the occasion when all the boarders in residence that week sat down together, Kevin pushed off back to the shop to deal with his regular correspondents and to compile the personal astrological charts.

He always wore his Vanda garb on the job: a yellow kaftan splashed with black squiggles plus the gold turban and hoop earrings. He did go easy on the make-up, finding, from experience, that a couple of hours toiling over the stove played hell with the false eyelashes, but the Vanda disguise helped to put him in the mood for the Sunday afternoon stint.

It was a miserable afternoon, the sky slatey, the unearthly glimmer from his computer screen lending an eeriness to the cramped quarters, muted background music from a radio stashed under the brocade cloth covering the table hardly intruding at all.

Kevin worked away until the room was almost in darkness and finally, pushing his forecasts into anonymous brown envelopes, he stamped each one and stuffed them into his shoulder bag.

Madame Vanda's consulting rooms, as the woman downstairs insisted on calling them, were Kevin's only hideaway, his existence at Leslie's and for three evenings a week at the club being conducted in the full glare of raucous scrutiny. The rooms he rented from Mrs Chater comprised kitchenette, toilet and a pseudo sitting room tricked out in velvet drapes, a Turkish rug and, apart from a shaded lamp on the table, the only lighting was a forest of candles and nightlights cunningly concealed in red glass jars.

He made himself a pot of tea and sat by the window listening to the early evening footsteps of strollers making their way along the street below. Sunday afternoons were an oasis, the calm waters in which his public persona could quench an aching thirst. He needed to think. Needed to make a move. Leaving Leslie's would be a wrench, shedding Madame Vanda would be like being skinned alive, leaving the naked Kevin Last exposed for what he was: a bald, frightened man nearing thirty, on the edge of a void.

His bank manager, a Mr Frankland, had been encouraging, the tweed jacket and pony-tail wig supporting this proposed change of career. Naturally, the old wet blanket felt it his professional duty to warn his customer of the pitfalls of investing in restaurants but, as luck would have it, he and Mrs Frankland were regular customers at Le Pendu and, admiring Barker's menus, he felt confident that, in the right hands, the bistro could be turned around in six months.

"It's a flourishing location, Mr Last, and with all the redevelopment on the South Bank, things can only get better. We knew Mr Ferguson quite well as it happens. His death in such terrible circumstances shocked my wife and I to the core. We would be sorry to see Mr Barker sell up but your participation could save the day. The accountant I recommended has been guardedly optimistic. Your estate agent in Birmingham anticipates a quick sale?"

"Absolutely. That's why we fixed on a sensible selling price. In fact, my tenant, who has been living in the house since my grandmother died, has already put in a bid."

"A satisfactory offer I hope? I would not wish you to be carried away just to get a quick sale. We have already agreed the overdraft you asked for and the Birmingham property is, I understand, in a prominent part of town."

"Selling the place presents no problems. Finding a flat to rent here in London might be difficult. But my landlady at the shop says I can use my rooms upstairs as living accommodation until something turns up."

Mr Frankland nodded sagely, aware that his customer's healthy balance was buoyed up by "design consultancy work", a nebulous description but Mr Last's consistently businesslike association with the bank, a rare enough commodity among "arty" types, gave Head Office no qualms about the proposed loan, backed up as it was with Kevin's savings, a not inconsiderable nest egg accrued from his cabaret performances, the cash payment basis of which remained a secret between Kevin and Syd Kelly of Kelly's Klub.

"Of course, in view of the proposed refurbishment at Le Pendu, it would assist me considerably if you could recruit another backer, someone with experience of the restaurant trade. Mr Ferguson was' in consultation with another investor you say?"

"Mr Toomey got cold feet after the attack. Mr Ferguson was recommended to him by our wine merchant the chef tells me."

"Perhaps you could re-approach this gentleman. Put your cards on the table. With the adjusted finances and a viable business plan I feel sure any experienced investor would think again. A third partner would make all the difference, Mr Last. I don't mean to criticise your own abilities but may I assume that the restaurant business is not your usual line of work?"

Kevin lay on the small sofa in his rooms above the shop recalling this nerve-racking encounter at the bank, relieved to find that Mr Frankland not only took him seriously but considered Le Pendu a commercial venture worth a gamble. But he was right. A third leg would make the whole structure much more stable, and when he had repeated Mr Frankland's suggestion to Terry Barker the chef had agreed with him.

"Never met this Toomey bloke myself but being a regular at the Savoy Grill can't be bad. The doorman remembered him like a shot when the police were asking about poor Jimmy's last movements that night. Worth a try. Get on to Ray Colthorpe at the wine warehouse. He was the one what introduced Jimmy to Toomey in the first place, see if he'll put in a good word for you. At least the guy's been over the books before, knows all the wrinkles and only wants to be a sleeping partner. Be a sight easier than trawling round for a new backer who knows nothing about us and would probably want to put his oar in on the general running of the place. You're a smart boy, Kevin, and with your gift of the gab I bet you could pull Toomey back on track. Get him here for a meal one night and I'll put on a three star menu. Rent a mob if you like, get some of those hooray henries here on a freebee with their gels, make the place look all the rage."

Kevin washed up the crocks, put on his trenchcoat and turned out the lights, locking up the shop with all the excessive care of a man who even saw bleak forebodings at the bottom of teacups. He posted his letters and caught a cab back to Brixton, fixing his lipstick in the mirror of his compact, rubbing a fleck off his teeth. Maybe ditching Madame Vanda on top of everything else was going too far. It was on a par with giving up the day job. The money would come in handy till he could see clear blue water between himself and Leslie's – it would allow him to sheer off from the Thursday, Friday and Saturday night shuffle and grind at Kelly's Klub.

Twenty-One

While Kevin was immersed in his star forecasts, Sylvie and Ian were finishing off a late lunch at the Old Spotted Cow.

"Are you off the Ferguson investigation now?"

"I think so. Until something new turns up anyhow. Frankly, unless an informant turns in the killer it's a long shot. The best chance would be a slot on one of the TV crime buster appeals but as we haven't even got a video recording of the crime there's nothing to go on. With all the surveillance equipment in shops and banks it's easier to nab a real robber than a hit and run chancer like this one."

"But public opinion is up in arms, the media has gone berserk decrying the thinness of policing, blathering on about homeless drifters and violence on the streets. Doesn't that make it easier to put on a supreme effort?"

"A botched mugging's not going to hog the headlines for more than two or three days at most. It's not as if the victim was a handsome lad with a brilliant career in front of him – a pretty girl, now, that would command some political clout."

"And I thought that sort of cynicism only raised its ugly head when votes were on the line."

Sylvie tossed down the dregs of her coffee and checked her watch.

"Ian, sorry to break this up but I've got to go."

He reached across the table and gripped her wrist.

Vivien Armstrong

"Not yet. Please? Just another hour. When's your rehearsal?"

"Six," she lied, smiling, smiling, smiling, her lips taut as a gag.

"A quickie then? I'll pay the bill while you're packing."

She relaxed, her dark eyes warm as pansies.

"OK."

It was after four before she drew up outside Fiona's town house in the city, a parking spot at the kerbside a bonus of the last Sunday before a new intake of undergraduates moved in.

Fiona greeted her with anxious hugs, her cable-knit sweater and leggings anticipating chilly days though, in fact, it was still warm enough to sit outside. She had laid tea on a garden table, two orange painted wicker chairs drawn up to a formal placement of bone china and sponge cake reminiscent of pre-war tennis parties as depicted in Bloomsbury still life pictures.

"Good God, Fifi. You didn't make the cake yourself, did you?"

"No, Megs did it. Loves cooking, that girl."

Megan was Fiona's sister, a theatre nurse at Addenbrookes who shared the house.

Sylvie plumped down in one of the chairs, admiring the pretty courtyard setting with its surviving windblown hanging baskets and yellow climbing roses on the trellis. Fiona had gone indoors to boil the kettle, and off-stage rattles of the pot-warming ritual reminded Sylvie how very far from home she really was.

She let Fiona fuss with the pastry forks and plates, and girly chit-chat yawned between what they both knew was the real bit of indigestion: the anonymous letter.

At last, after her second cup of tea and fulsome congratulations on the cream cake, Sylvie felt the time was ripe for broaching the subject. Fiona was clearly unnerved

146

by the melodramatic missive and was in no mood for light banter. She pulled the letter in its plain envelope from her briefcase which had lain like a sleeping tiger under the garden table.

Sylvie scanned the unsavoury item with scant enthusiasm and turned to Fiona.

"Well, it's a funny thing to send, I agree. But it's not exactly threatening, is it, Fifi?"

"I think I should hand it to the police."

"Why?"

"I don't like stuff like that pushed through my letter box – it could have been dog shit."

Sylvie grinned. "Believe me, the cops won't divert any patrol car here because of this. I don't think it's even technically 'chargeable' – if that's the legal term."

"Won't you show it to Ian for me?"

"He's gone back to Suffolk. Anyway, it's just a jazzed up message. If the same words had been typed up and sent as an e-mail you wouldn't have wasted a moment's anxiety on it. It's just because all these cut-out bits look so ghastly. Whoever sent it must have been raised on Boys' Own Paper guff. It's positively antediluvian, Fifi. By tomorrow you'll be laughing your head off about it. Anyway, where is Bonningstone?"

"I looked it up. There's one in Norfolk and one in Sussex. Take your pick."

"You don't seriously think I'm going to carry out these mad directions, do you? Sounds like a kids' treasure hunt clue. Once I get to this churchyard I'll find a second cobbled-together message ordering me to go on yet another wild goose chase. Putting flowers on the grave of a child I don't even know, even supposing the grave actually exists, is absolutely cockeyed. It doesn't even give me her full name – I'd have to ask Kevin to look in his crystal ball for me."

"Who's Kevin?"

147

"Never mind. Just a joke."

"But you honestly don't know the story?"

"Adele's involvement in this school trip accident? No, she never mentioned it. When she was teaching I was much younger and I imagine it was something she wanted to forget. How old was this unfortunate kid?"

"About fifteen I think. Adele and James Ferguson were in charge of a cycling tour in Brittany and . . ."

Sylvie jerked to attention, spilling tea in her lap.

"Ferguson? The guy who was mugged? Bloody hell."

Fiona nodded, warming to her narrative.

"It was a summer outing – I don't remember the details – but a group from this private school where Adele was employed set off with a bunch of boys and girls and a mini-bus. As far as I remember they were touring, staying at different hostels each night, the mini-bus driver and the school matron going ahead with all the luggage."

"How did the child die? In a traffic accident?"

"No, worse. The girl got detached from the rest of the party somehow and was later found dead. Murdered."

"Was anyone charged?"

"Yes. A local man, educationally sub-normal but until then considered harmless. Trouble was the Matron had it in for Adele, railed on about her carelessness in looking after the girls in the party. Adele had to leave."

"And Ferguson?"

"He got severely reprimanded by the French examining magistrate and ultimately got the sack."

"But it was an accident. Could have happened to a local child at any time if this French guy was a borderline case. Was she raped?"

Fiona shrugged. "I honestly can't remember but if I had been Adele I could never have put it out of my mind. A thing like that would haunt you, wouldn't it, even though you knew it was not your fault? I felt bad enough when my dog was run over," she added, biting her lip.

Sylvie leaned back, hugging her arms to her chest, suddenly feeling a chill breeze raise the hairs on her bare arms.

"That thing about me putting heather on the grave," she said, "rings a bell. When the contents of Adele's room were listed there was a bouquet of white heather. They asked me if I wanted it kept with her personal things. It meant nothing to me and everyone assumed it was something either given to her by a grateful client or a lucky talisman she bought for herself. Supposing she was keeping her fingers crossed that Underwood would come up trumps with the country house deal that weekend? Does that sound like Adele to you – some sort of good luck charm?"

Fiona looked dubious, shaking her head in disbelief. "Adele wasn't like that – she made her own luck. Tell you what. Suppose Adele still felt vaguely guilty after all these years, guilty about her own part in the girl's death? If she happened to be near the churchyard in Norfolk that weekend, it would be a nice gesture to put flowers on the grave herself, wouldn't it?"

"She was based in East Anglia. For all we know she left flowers on the grave every year on the anniversary of the girl's death. If it was a school summer trip it was probably in August. Adele wasn't totally hard hearted despite her bad press. What do you think?"

They looked at each other, both mystified by the possible motive Adele harboured in buying these flowers, wondering what purpose lay behind their purchase.

Sylvie made up her mind. "Look, Fiona, I'm absolutely booked up solid for the whole of next week. Final rehearsals. Once I've got an hour to spare I *will* search out this churchyard in Bonningstone if only to satisfy my curiosity but it sticks in my craw to be running up some blind alley at the behest of an anonymous scandalmonger.

Leave it with me," she said, holding out her hand for the envelope.

"OK. If you say so."

"Actually, I'm not that concerned about the bloody letter. I think I can guess who sent it."

"Who?"

"Can't say till I find out more but I promise you I'll get to the bottom of it without involving the police."

"Why don't you want to share this with Ian?"

"Because he would only take the official line and, frankly, not only would that be a total waste of time but it would also muddy the waters in the Ferguson enquiry which is out of his hands. I'll let you into a secret."

Fiona stiffened, all eyes.

"I did an absolutely terrible thing which you, as a lawyer, will blanch at. I rifled through Ian's case notes while he was sleeping."

"Oh, great! That's all I need. You've probably done something listed under the Official Secrets Act and I, as a willing accomplice, will be struck off!" Fiona was not altogether joking.

"I only took a peek, didn't steal anything. There was nothing about this school trip tragedy on which the French files must have been closed years ago. Anyway, I got Ferguson's ex-wife's address. I shall go and see her. Offer my condolences and pose a few questions of my own."

"As Adele's sister? Are you completely raving, Sylvie? The woman's marriage was ruined by their carrying on at the school. It hit every tabloid in the country at the time. Utterly humiliating for her. Why should she confide in *you*?"

"I've got another angle. A friend of mine is putting his life's savings into Ferguson's restaurant and I would like to get her candid opinion about it. Do you think she can claim his share in the business?"

"Tricky question. Are there children involved?"

"Can't say. All I know is she's never remarried so presumably Ferguson's been paying alimony for years. I can also ask her about this child murder in France – she may still have some press cuttings or something."

"Sylvie, the woman's going to slam the door in your face. What makes you think you can infiltrate her home so soon after her ex-husband's been killed and quiz her about her personal finances?"

Sylvie grinned, grabbing up her tote bag and stuffing the offending letter inside.

"Charm, ducky. Oscar-winning theatrical charm. You'll see. I'll ring you next weekend, shall I?"

Twenty-Two

K evin togged himself up in a new blazer and corduroys to call on Ray Colthorpe, the wine supplier to Le Pendu. Terry Barker had phoned ahead introducing his potential new partner and Kevin psyched himself up to face the key man himself.

The warehouse was in Southwark, close to the river and not all that far from the restaurant. He was nervous, well aware that his knowledge of wine was never enough to pass any expert's test, and knowing that bullshitting Colthorpe was a waste of time.

The ramshackle building boosted his confidence and Kevin consoled himself that, having overcome the bank hurdle which to his mind was much more of a challenge, forming a business relationship with the wine merchant was "small beer", an inappropriate cliche which put a smile on his face as he knocked at the door of Colthorpe's office and walked in.

The place was pretty shambolic, folders littering the desk and piled on top of the filing cabinet. A middle-aged secretary smiled encouragement at the fresh-faced young man hovering in the doorway as Colthorpe rose from his chair and extended a warm handshake.

Colthorpe was fiftyish, tall and with the long nose and florid complexion of a man who lived for the job. He was in his shirtsleeves and sported red braces and a modest paunch, the jacket of what was clearly an expensive bespoke suit on a coathanger on a hatstand behind the door.

Kevin accepted the seat Colthorpe indicated and launched into his rehearsed spiel, the older man watching intently over spectacles perched way down the long nose. Barker had filled in Kevin with the details of the business with Colthorpe and admitted that it was Ferguson that had been the sommelier. He also told Kevin that Colthorpe had always insisted on prompt payment for his high quality wines.

Colthorpe heard him out, studying the accountant's résumé of the current financial situation at Le Pendu and the business plan which Kevin had expertly concocted on his computer. The wholesaler had been in the business all his life and prized his ability to spot a "flanneller" and said so, quite brusquely, leaving Kevin under no illusion that his arrival on the restaurant scene would be greeted with circumspection.

"Now, look here, Kevin. I may call you Kevin, may I not? Let's be frank. I've always had a high regard for Terry Barker and would like to help you. But I get the impression that you're a bit green when it comes down to it. Fair comment?"

Kevin nodded, flushing painfully, well aware that creating an association with a new wine merchant would be difficult if not impossible, even allowing for Terry Barker's good name in the trade and the fact that Ferguson had always paid his supplier promptly, leaving no nasty aftertaste in the wine dealers' close circle despite the rumours that Le Pendu had a cash flow problem.

Colthorpe carried on, his eyes steely. "I've been in this business too many years to be swayed by sentiment but, between you and me, Kevin, I have a high regard for my old friend Terry and I'd hate to see Le Pendu go down. Losing Jimmy Ferguson in that terrible way knocked Terry for six, and losing Toomey's investment could not have come at a worse time. Terry tells me you intend to romance Toomey again, see if he'll reconsider?"

"I need someone who knows about wine. We *can* manage without his financial input but it would be a struggle. If Mr Toomey could at least be persuaded to come back on board in an advisory capacity at first we would be appreciative. If he also agreed to put some capital in to back up his judgement we would be killing two birds with one stone. If not, Terry and I may have to cast about for a new backer, someone in the trade, and that someone might overbalance a partnership that is barely on its feet to start with. You see our problem, Mr Colthorpe? If you could see your way to recommend us to Mr Toomey your word would, I know, carry enormous weight."

"Jimmy suffered from being too confident in choosing wines for Le Pendu. That, if I may say so, is not your problem and if we are to re-establish contact your honesty in that respect does you credit. If Toomey refuses to come aboard you would have to rely on *my* recommendations in purchasing, do you see? Terry trusts me but I would wish to rectify some very expensive errors Jimmy insisted on making, errors which are still clogging your cellar, am I not right?"

Kevin nodded.

"I warned Jimmy about the wine list he was determined to construct. Le Pendu appeals to a clientele for whom chateau-bottled wines are too pricy and, as a newcomer to the trade, looking after such pampered long-term residents of your cellar would certainly present problems for you. Are you with me?"

Kevin blinked, accepting the older man's advice in good spirit.

"How much do you know about Toomey?"

Kevin cleared his throat and launched into a summary of the background information Terry had run through with him.

Colthorpe listened patiently, nodding at intervals and smiling like a Chinese mandarin. Inscrutable.

As Kevin's words dried up, Colthorpe leaned back in his leather armchair and weighed up his options. At last, after what seemed an interminable silence, he started to speak, his voice lowered almost to a whisper.

"Toomey's been in prison."

"Yes, I know that. For fraud. Terry said it was unimportant."

"Terry told you the whole story?"

"Not exactly."

"Well, if you and I are going to do business together it is necessary, Kevin, dear boy, that you are fully in the picture. Can you taste the difference between a 1982 Le Pin and a £5 bottle of Australian chardonnay?"

Kevin shrugged.

"You're not the only one, lad. Le Pendu has never, even with Jimmy's high-flown intentions, been in the same league as the fraud for which Toomey was convicted. Make no mistake about it, Toomey's still a good friend of mine and he never, never once, tried to cheat me. The fakes Toomey concocted were never crude and his customers were, thank God, mostly to be found in Hong Kong. Wine forgery is on the increase and some wily collectors of the top quality produce have been known to test the knowledge of their suppliers with bottles known to be fakes. Toomey kept me up front with the scams I might be a victim of even with my experience, and once or twice a month he brought in some samples to see if I thought them passable. He poured two glasses of a so-called Mouton 1945 for us on one occasion – knew I would spot it but wanted to show me how it was done, explained the business of old bottles, old labels and so on. We had a bit of a laugh and then cracked a decent bottle of champagne to rinse the tonsils."

Colthorpe lit a cigar and sat hunched over the desk, smiling to himself, absorbed in some kind of private reverie. Kevin waited, knowing when to hold his tongue, and after a moment the older man continued.

"All this is strictly between ourselves, you understand. Toomey was a player of world class in a wicked trade which is conservatively estimated to be worth as much as twelve million a year. It's a nightmare. He could even supply a provenance if required, a history of the wine's trail from collector to collector. Toomey was one of the best and made an uncalculable fortune out of it."

"How did he get caught?"

Colthorpe frowned. "Some bloody whistleblower set up an elaborate trap. Don't take me wrong, I'm as glad as the next man when fakers are revealed, it's death to this business, but Toomey and I were pals. I knew what he was up to and he knew I'd turn a blind eye so long as he never tried to foist a single bottle of fakery on me. I liked the man. And I wasn't the only one who was sorry to see him banged up. A scoundrel, I admit, but don't we all love a charming villain? And the snobs who traded in his wares were never drinking the stuff, didn't even enjoy wine of that class if you ask me – it was a collectors' market, mostly Far Eastern buyers who wouldn't know a Chateau Margaux from a bottle of Tizer. One poor Jap didn't even spot spelling mistakes on the labels, they'd even printed duff *appellation d'origine* on his consignment and he paid up, happy as a sandboy. But Toomey was a master, would never be caught out by stupid mistakes like that and, between a few wrong cases, he was trading high quality stuff, mixing and fixing we called it." Colthorpe grinned at the recollection like an old soldier reminiscing about battles long ago.

"But are you still in touch with Mr Toomey? He's still trading?"

"Retired. Living on his ill-gotten gains, shouldn't wonder. Truth is Toomey's never been the same since he got out of prison. Lives alone in this big place on the coast, comes in here from time to time to share a bottle, but the light's gone out of the man."

"But you were the one to suggest to Ferguson that he approach him?"

"Why not? I thought it was time my old friend shook himself, took an interest in life. Being part of Le Pendu struck me as something that would make all the difference. As it happens he already knew of it, had already mentioned it to me a couple of times, quizzed me about Terry Barker's previous kitchens. He had a nose for a potential winner and I knew they were looking for some cash input and, after a bit of pushing, he agreed to hear what Jimmy had to say for himself. Ferguson being killed like that frightened Toomey off. With his record he needed to keep a low profile, didn't want the police nosing about thinking he was up to his old tricks, infiltrating the wine trade by the back door."

The secretary came in with a stack of letters to sign.

"Thank you, Molly. Would you be an angel and bring my friend and I a bottle of Mouton Rothschild and some glasses? Bless you."

When she had gone Kevin plucked up courage to ask the question.

"Have you decided, Mr Colthorpe? Will you speak to Mr Toomey on our behalf, ask him to see me at least, give me a chance to explain the new situation?"

Colthorpe nodded. "But just assure me, Kevin my boy, assure me that you are under no illusions about this man? I take it Terry is in full agreement with you? He knows that Toomey's been inside but is not conversant with my undercover support of the scoundrel while he was plying his nefarious trade. Your discretion in this aspect is vitally important to me. Some members of my fraternity got badly burned by Toomey's game and are unforgiving. My personal sympathies are a private matter between us two, agreed?"

Before he could answer, Molly came back with the wine and Colthorpe hurried round the desk to accept the tray. A hushed silence ensued while he performed the exquisite ritual of uncorking the bottle, pouring a little to admire the rich hue, dipping his long nose into the goblet to savour the aroma, and finally to taste, his eyes closing in pleasure.

Kevin sat mutely, blessing whatever lucky star had inexplicably shone on his appeal to this streetwise trader, whatever magic had persuaded the man to take this stranger into his confidence. Colthorpe poured a second glass and reverently passed it to him.

In silence they toasted their bond and when they had sealed this new association, Colthorpe scribbled an address on a memo pad and passed it over, smiling in that enigmatic way which both puzzled and confirmed Kevin's trust in the man.

"I will ring him this evening when I get home, give you my blessing. As we have been so frank with each other, Kevin, may I ask a personal question?"

Kevin nodded, suddenly anxious about his wig.

Colthorpe narrowed his eyes. "Tell me, young man, what was your line of business before deciding to run a restaurant?"

Kevin looked him straight in the eye.

"Fortune telling."

The older man roared with laughter, tossing down the final dregs of the wine in his glass. "Ask no questions, be told no lies, as my old nanny used to say," he crowed, cheerfully unconvinced by what was, in fact, the truest of confidences.

Twenty-Three

N ext morning Sylvie ambushed Kevin in the kitchen before it was light, knowing him to be the only other boarding house resident who rose with the lark. He was busy at the chopping board, dissecting kidneys. Sylvie winced, averting her eyes from the bloody pulp between his fingers.

"Hi, Sylvie. Couldn't sleep?"

"My best chance of catching you on your own, sweetie. We haven't had a chance to talk for days. Any news on the restaurant front?"

His eyes lit up. "Yeah, terrific! The bank's given the thumbs up to a new overdraft, I've accepted an offer on my house and I've told Leslie I'm leaving at the end of the month."

"Wow! Really? You're no slouch, Kevin Last, I'll give you that. How did Leslie take it?"

"A bit shocked. We've been together nine years, you know. But he guessed something was up when I stopped wearing the turban at home and took all my Vanda outfits to the club. I can use a cupboard in one of Kelly's dressing rooms. Means I can keep that side of things private."

"Where will you live?"

"Over the shop till I've found my feet."

"Still doing the tarot readings?"

"Only by appointment after three in the afternoons. Just until I know the restaurant's up and running." He tossed the kidneys into a pan with some mushrooms while she

159

made some toast. "Coffee's on the stove. Help yourself," he said, his bald pate gleaming under the spotlight above the stove.

They sat down together and Sylvie switched to a lighter vein, describing the catty infighting at Garnett's now that the final rehearsals were under way.

"Will you come to First Night, Kevin? We could make up a party. You, me, Ian Preston that policeman I've been dating, and Fiona plus any man she can rustle up for the evening. It's only a small venue in Battersea, not much more than a tryout before we move on to Bristol, but it might be fun. What do you say?"

"Sure, sounds wonderful. But fun? Not a load of laughs from what I've heard about this Ibsen guy. Melville, the comedian with the ginger hair who was here till last week, was telling me about this play you're in. A classic he said. About time I got some culture," he added with a wry grin.

Sylvie laughed, tucking into her scrambled eggs, wondering if it was too soon to ask Kevin how the other boarders had taken to his transformation from Vanda to this good looking young man with the fashionably shaven head of a style victim.

She tested their friendship on a general question about his parents. He seemed unfazed by her curiosity, explaining that, in fact, he had largely been brought up in care.

"Had a couple of foster parent stints but it didn't work out. I was a difficult kid, pretty violent in those days and skiving off school every chance I got. I was lucky not to get caught shoplifting or I might have been well on the road to ruin by now."

"Poor kid. You never got visits from your people?"

"My mum used to turn up from time to time but she sort of faded out when I got older and got bolshy. I never knew my dad and never bothered to track down any relatives so you could say I was a bit of an oddball

160

from the start. School was terrible. Got suspended twice, kicked out another time after trying to set fire to the lab, and if I hadn't gone down with the tumour when I was fifteen drugs were next on the cards. I was lucky."

"Getting a brain tumour was lucky?" Sylvie retorted, aghast at his aplomb, horrified by this unexpected picture of a rough, tough child bundled from foster parents to care institutions, from school to school.

"Going into hospital broke the chain, see. For once in my life *I* was the important one, nice people on my side, kind doctors persuading me that life wasn't so bad, especially when you're sharing a ward with kids who died on you."

"Good God, Kevin. What happened when you left hospital with no-one on your side just like before?"

"I bummed around. Lived rough one summer. Eventually got a job at a garden centre for a while. Then I met Leslie. He loved me, ugly, awkward little sod that I was. Leslie took over as the dad I never knew, looked after me, taught me to sing, got me a job at a club up Streatham way. Made more dough in a month than I knew what to do with. And later I had this solicitor's letter saying this lady in Birmingham had left her house and all her money to me. Said she was my grandmother, left me a whole load of photo albums and letters. My mum had been killed in a car crash I found out, and the grannie I never knew was too embarrassed to contact me while she was alive. I'll show you her picture if you like. Nice looking old bird, very straight-laced I'd imagine and lived in a smart part of the city. Felt guilty about the way me and Mum had been shoved under the carpet she told the solicitor when she made the will. But she knew about me all along, just couldn't face up to the neighbours' talk. Could have visited me in hospital if she'd been a real Christian, couldn't she? Leaving me her money after she was dead was the easy option. That's why I've got no worries about chucking it away on a failed restaurant if it comes to it. Fate dropped it in my lap, fate can take it away."

Sylvie stared, open-mouthed. "You sad bastard. No wonder you started searching for good luck in your stars."

"The astrology? The caretaker at Kelly's Klub got me interested first off. A silly old cow called Beryl Wall. Kept us all in fits with her star sign fixations. I couldn't believe she somehow got it right but stuff she spewed out turned up trumps time after time, so I got myself a proper tutor in Bethnel Green. Cost a packet at the time but that's how Madame Vanda got started and between you and me, Sylv, I've made a sizeable packet from the game, mostly from my regulars who write in or ring me up at the shop with their little worries. Hang on my every word, God bless 'em. I haven't forgotten our deal you know. I gave up the turban like you said but you still haven't got around to that tarot reading I promised you."

"Well, we've been a bit busy lately, haven't we, Kevin? Actually, I've got something weird to show you. See if you can sense any vibes," she said, not altogether in jest, producing the anonymous letter dropped off at Fiona's house.

She made fresh coffee while he studied the nasty piece of paper, now distinctly dog-eared from its travels in Sylvie's tote bag. Kevin held it delicately between long fingers innocent of the usual nail extensions, and then touched the letter with his lips, his eyes closed.

After a moment he roused himself and passed it back. "This sort of dirt's normally a woman's trick if you'll excuse the awful generalisation, but not this. The bloke who sent this is no fool – but clearly ten pence short of a shilling as they say. Watch out, Sylvie love, I sense real danger here. Don't go."

She giggled, snatching back the letter and stuffing it back in her bag.

"My sentiments exactly, Svengali. Even if I had the

time to pedal round Norfolk looking for this kid's grave, I wouldn't give the sender the satisfaction. But, in an oblique way, I *am* going on a wild goose chase of a sort. I've phoned Ferguson's widow and she's agreed to see me on Friday after the dress rehearsal."

Kevin was stunned. "Why?"

She shrugged. "Idle curiosity. Plus wanting to make sure you're not throwing your money down the drain in this restaurant game. For all you know, Mrs Ferguson's going to claim a chunk of Le Pendu for herself, especially if she finds out it's being relaunched with a cash injection from a young man with, let's face it, the business sense of a newt. I feel responsible, Kevin. It was me who first got you into this."

He smiled, not bothered by her candour, knowing Sylvie to be a true friend whatever reservations she held about his ability to make money which, in fact, was his forte. Even his bank manager acknowledged this fact though the mysterious source of his income was unclear.

He said, "I'm going to see Toomey, the original prospective third partner."

"You're not serious? Does your crystal ball not warn you, my lad, that Toomey's a crook? He's been inside. For fraud," she persisted.

"I know. The wine merchant told me the whole story. But I *need* someone who knows wine, Sylvie. Toomey is familiar with our set-up at Le Pendu, Terry likes him and he's not going to muscle in on the running of the place. If he agrees to reconsider his decision to back off, Terry and I will get a proper legal agreement pasted up. Belt and braces, I promise you. No need to go to see Ferguson's wife on my behalf, really there isn't."

"It's not just about the restaurant. I've only just found out about this child murder in France. It happened years ago. Fiona's forgotten half the details – this woman Pamela Ferguson can fill in the rest for me." Sylvie told him the whole story as far as she had ascertained from Fiona. "I need to know everything, Kevin. Why did Adele keep quiet about such a ghastly crime? What else but guilt would make her continue to put flowers on the grave? Was Adele more involved than anyone knew?"

"Flowers on the grave?"

"Heather. White heather. Out of season in August, too, so my tame florist tells me. That makes it an expensive gesture."

Kevin looked thoughtful, but before he could question her again Leslie burst into the kitchen grinning from ear to ear, his scraggy frame wrapped in Kevin's candlewick dressing gown.

"Birds of a feather, I see," he chortled, kissing Kevin's bald head with a loud smack of the lips. "He told you he's flying the nest too, lovey? Leaving poor old Leslie to catch his own early worms?" The tone was light but an underlying bitterness alerted Sylvie that her presence at Leslie's would not, in future, be welcome. She rose to go, tall as a tree, winking at Kevin over Leslie's shoulder, reminding him to keep Saturday night free for her opening night.

"Would you like a ticket, Leslie? Shall I leave half a dozen on the hallstand for the boys?"

"My boys are all working Saturday nights, dearie. As Kevin ought to be if he's got any sense. Kelly won't stand for any drama queen tactics, my lad," he added with a sour twist to what started out as a grin.

Sylvie left them to it, certain Kevin in his turbanless persona and growing maturity was entirely capable of managing the rest of his life without campy old has-beens like Leslie Geroni.

Twenty-Four

Rehearsals were running at fever pitch by the end of the week. Since Joanna's elevation to flavour of the month on Harry Garnett's menu, her confidence had soared to prima donna status and the unexpected bits of business she slipped into the performance flicked the old stagers on the raw, not least Sylvie despite having programmed herself to skate through this production without getting involved in the in-fighting.

Costumes were an irritation and actors, being nothing if not narcissistic, were put out by the ratty wardrobe service. Sylvie, topping the leading lady by several inches, had trained herself to cringe on stage as far as the character of Mrs Elvsted allowed which, in fact, fitted in quite nicely under the harsh glare of Hedda's polite scorn, but her own ensemble was as unflattering as any she had ever been called upon to wear even on Garnett's tight budget.

The wardrobe mistress did her best, taking in the excess and casting round for a corset that actually fitted, but the colour was all wrong, the drab brown doing nothing for Sylvie's dark complexion. Joanna's costumes were beautifully tailored with flattering military touches of braid and her fair colouring bloomed against the jewel tones of the Edwardian dresses.

"I look as sallow as a corn-fed chicken in this," Sylvie blurted out on stage, her eyes sparking with discontent.

"Perhaps you *are* bloody sallow," Harry fumed, having

already had a bellyful from his leading man whose boots were a size too small.

But she had to smile, her natural good temper getting the better of her when the sound of Rory prancing about on the boards in his squeaky boots caused a tearful outburst from Joanna who was convinced he was doing it on purpose just to wreck her delivery.

Sylvie was glad to get away. Her anxiety to be on time for her appointment with Ferguson's widow doused further niggling complaints about the way Joanna was still ad libbing on stage – throwing her off balance with unrehearsed moves which, to Sylvie's mind and the smug amusement of the rest of the cast, were undoubtedly unprofessional at this late stage.

Pamela Ferguson's response to Sylvie's phone call had been guarded but she had sportingly agreed to spare half an hour on Friday evening to discuss Sylvie's alleged proposed investment in Le Pendu. She had said nothing about being Adele's sister and apart from formal condolences on her ex-husband's tragic death the conversation had been businesslike.

The semi-detached house in Dulwich Village was a pretty family residence in the smart end of South London and not that far at all from the rehearsal rooms. Whatever matrimonial settlement had been made, Ferguson had clearly been generous but who knows, she reflected, perhaps Pamela Ferguson had money of her own and, after all these years since their divorce, presumably pulled in a decent salary to boot.

Sylvie parked right outside confident that in such a leafy suburb as this her little hire car was in no danger of a break-in, not that there was anything worth smashing a window for, not yet having even got round to organising a mobile phone for herself, much to Ian's irritation.

Pamela opened the door, a hall light silhouetting a slim figure in a tailored suit. Sylvie, straight from work, immediately felt dusty and unkempt, wishing she had had time to make herself decent before hurrying to keep this appointment.

The woman was friendly enough and the house homely, funky music drifting downstairs from what Sylvie assumed was the children's rooms. Two, wasn't it? A girl and a boy she seemed to remember from Kevin's chance remarks. She followed Ferguson's widow into a sizeable living room, the product of two rooms combined at a guess, both ends furnished with fireplaces each set up on this fine October evening with a pot of hydrangeas.

She left Sylvie to herself while she fetched the coffee and to shout up the stairs to the music buff in the attic to turn down the volume. She returned almost immediately with the tray, the coffee perked on cue it would seem. Sylvie now realised promptitude had been a wise move.

As soon as preliminary introductions had been completed and Sylvie had made excuses for her jeans and sweatshirt, they settled either side of the hearth. Sylvie described her tight rehearsal schedule, chatting on about the difficulties small companies such as Garnett's Rep experienced. Her listener softened up by degrees, clearly fascinated by the problems of selling Ibsen to small provincial theatres with cash problems of their own.

"But what makes you think the restaurant business is a better bet?" she asked, genuinely puzzled.

"I have a little money to invest, I know the remaining partner and I like the style of Le Pendu. Perhaps you could say I'm a mug who likes to have a flutter, am conditioned to living on the edge."

"Well, I must warn you that James – my ex-husband – never made much of a profit from it. He could never accept that to make money in that line of business one has almost to be born to it. To James it was a dream. He used to be a teacher you know. Owning a restaurant was something he always wanted to do and when he won some money on the Lottery he splashed out and threw it into that leaky bucket."

"He won on the Lottery? Really? Goodness, I've never met anyone who managed to do that. Was it the jackpot?"

"About a quarter of a million. But that's only my guess. It was well after our divorce and as our parting was on a lump sum basis any savings James put into that crackpot scheme were his own affair."

"That's something I wanted to ask you. Please tell me to mind my own business if I'm being rude but you see it's important that I check any facts which Terry Barker tells me. He said you are making no claim on the restaurant even if it is re-financed and turns out to be a success. There is another potential backer beside myself and I feel we both need to be fully conversant with any possible future demands on Le Pendu."

"I quite understand, Sylvie. OK if I call you Sylvie? No, James was a lousy husband but an honest man and always generous to a fault. When we divorced he turned over all our matrimonial assets to me and made a final settlement plus a trust fund for our children. My daughter is a student at Durham and Samuel goes to school here in Dulwich, a day boy. So you see I would in no way have a lien on the restaurant nor would I wish to do so. Insisting on being a partner might involve me in a financial loss rather than a gain if I may say so," she said as an apologetic aside. "As it happens I'm fortunate enough to have my own career – an optician's business here in the Village and a branch in Bromley. When we parted I was at first very bitter and, I'm ashamed to admit, took James to the cleaners, practically emptied his back pockets from pure spite."

She smiled, her greying hair curling prettily around her face, the face of a woman now content with her lot.

"Would you like something stronger, Sylvie? Whisky? A glass of wine? It's so nice for me to have someone to chat to in the evening. Now that Samuel's a teenager his interests centre around the computer and music centre in his room, and who can blame him?"

"Whisky would be lovely. Thank you, Pamela."

Mrs ex-Ferguson pushed aside the coffee cups and set two tumblers on the table between them, easing off her shoes and curling up on the sofa, all girls together. Sylvie, who prided herself on a knack with casual friendships, was nevertheless surprised at the ease with which she had slipped into the woman's confidence.

"Are you married, Sylvie?"

"Still hoping," she replied with a grin.

"Shouldn't bother if I were you. Marriage brought me nothing but grief. Apart from my kids that is."

"Your husband was a teacher you said. Here in London?"

"No. At a private school near Eastbourne. Not an academically renowned establishment but the advantage for us was that a housemaster's cottage was included. Fortunately, we had managed to save some money living in, and my parents topped it up at the end when he got kicked out and the children and I found ourselves homeless."

"Dismissed? For what?"

Pamela Ferguson topped up her glass and Sylvie guessed that lonely drinking sessions were not unusual after her optician's place put up the shutters.

"Having an affair with a member of staff."

"A woman?"

Pamela laughed. "Oh, yes. James wasn't gay. Perhaps if he had been Finings House School might not have thrown us out. It was the femme fatale element that did it. But there was more to it, the governors were quite right to get rid of them both and everyone was perfectly decent to me, awfully sympathetic, but what could they do? It was all over the papers."

"An affair at a little private school. Surely not?"

She nodded. "Oh, it was worse than that. It was more than ten years ago, you must have read about it yourself at the time. A child died. Her body was brought back to England and buried near the school."

"I lived in Canada until recently, all this is news to me. A pupil died you say. And they blamed your husband?"

She nodded, gazing into the fireplace, on the face of it mesmerised by the blue hydrangeas.

"James taught French and German and the school had organised a cycling holiday in Brittany for some fifth formers and a few members of staff, including this young French teacher, the Matron and a couple of others, I forget who. It was only afterwards I learned that James had been having a passionate affair with this other teacher for months, everyone knew about it. He was absolutely smitten but I suppose they thought, on a school trip, they would cut it out, especially with Miss Forster in tow. The Matron was one of the old school, awfully down on that sort of thing, especially as the school was co-educational."

"Boarding?"

"Yes, of course. A lovely main building with its own estate and, although exam results weren't exactly brilliant, the fees were horrendous and right up until the girl's death on this trip the place had a wonderful reputation, no scandals about drugs or anything. A bit of bullying but we didn't know about that side of it until the police investigation dragged it all out into the open. According to the poor girl's only friend, a child called Jessica, Erica was desperately unhappy at school and kept phoning home begging to be allowed back from France. But her mother refused. Erica was a podgy child, you see, big for her age, just puppy fat I'm sure but her mother thought a fortnight's cycling would trim her down and also improve her French which her father paid extra for – she had individual tuition from James."

"So he knew her quite well? Realised how wretched she was?"

"Guessed as much but she seemed to find it impossible

to make friends and homesickness at a boarding school is something the staff tend to ignore."

"What happened?"

"Every day this bunch of kids would set off on their hired bikes and every day Erica got left behind. Everyone was irritated by her constant moaning and the trouble was James and his lady love were too engrossed in each other to keep an eye on her. One afternoon they got to the next hostel and found Erica was missing yet again. James and the mini-van driver went back over the route but couldn't find her and Matron hit the roof. Blamed Adele, the young teacher, for enticing my husband to neglect his duty – there were tales of skinny-dipping after dark, boys ogling at them from the windows of the hostel, all sorts of naughtiness. And when Erica vanished they thought at first she must have pushed off home on her own. The police were alerted but French country bobbies are no better than our own and it was another twenty-four hours before they mounted a proper search."

"But she hadn't run away?"

"Unfortunately not. The bike was discovered hidden in some bushes but Erica's body wasn't discovered for two days. She had been attacked, half strangled, raped and thrown into a river."

"Drowned?"

"Yes. If anyone had seen her in the water she might have been saved. They traced the attacker quite quickly – a mental case, a farm boy called Didier Varenne, I'll never forget it. He was tried and sentenced but really he was in no state to plead and they put him away."

"Did he say what happened?"

"He told them he was riding home from work on his bike and found her crying at the side of the road. Alone. Her tyre was punctured and she couldn't mend it. He promised to fix it for her and and removed the wheel, then said he needed some water from the river to test the inner tube. And when she went down the bank with him this crazy fellow admitted he asked her for a kiss. She struggled and it must have lit his fuse. He insisted he remembered nothing more but there was forensic evidence which led the cops to him and – I suppose – he was a local nutter and an obvious suspect. Anyway, for once, the French police got it right, arrested Varenne, got a confession and James and Adele faced censure for their lack of care. James admitted everything, of course, took the entire blame and offered to resign which was a formality in the circumstances. I demanded a divorce and he was agreeable which was sad. In retrospect, I felt we should have given it time to heal. But when your husband's blatent affair with a younger woman is splashed all over the tabloids and discussed on TV, one's humiliation is made so much worse by everyone insisting on giving an opinion, never leaving one alone for a moment. Also poor James really thought she was in love with him you know. She went back to her husband immediately and James never got over it, loved that little cock-teaser right to the end. We were friends eventually, James and I, and he's really been a kind and loving parent all along. He used to come here every weekend for Samuel and later we'd often pick over the old wounds."

She sipped her whisky, almost unconscious of Sylvie's rapt attention.

"After we were forced to leave the school he was unemployable as a teacher, of course. The publicity was awful and I wasn't forgiving like Adele's other half. She just walked away, dusted herself down and left the two of us tearing at each other's throats. James had to take odd jobs for years until he won this lottery pay-out and bought into the restaurant. He admitted recently that he had caught up with Adele again and, like a mutt, harboured no grievances despite the fact that she had broken his heart, destroyed his marriage and ruined his career in teaching. Can you believe it?"

"They became lovers once more?"

"Apparently not. And James wouldn't bother to lie to me these days. He spotted her website and realised she was probably in a position to lend him some money, purely on a business footing, until he could find an extra partner for Le Pendu. Adele was a cold-hearted bitch to the end, agreed to bail him out but was going to charge extortionate interest on the loan – it was no gift from the heart, believe me."

"I'm afraid I haven't been entirely straight about Adele. I knew about her affair with your husband. She died you know."

Pamela's hand flew to her mouth. "No!"

"You never heard? A swimming pool accident a little while ago."

Sylvie rose to go but Pamela remained slumped in the corner of the sofa, her eyes glazed with shock.

"Did James know?"

"Must have done."

"He never mentioned it to me. Are you sure it was Adele Morrison?"

"Absolutely certain. Look, as I said, I'm here under false pretences. If I'd told you the whole truth I'm sure you would have refused to see me. But because of my friend I *was* really worried about your financial interest in the restaurant and I was genuinely unaware until recently about the death of the schoolgirl. I needed to know everything about Adele for my own peace of mind and you are the only person I could ask. Did you keep any press cuttings?"

She shook her head, utterly confused, even a little frightened, steadying herself against the sideboard as she stood to face this stranger she had invited into her house. Sylvie realised that the poor soul had clearly had a drink or two before she had knocked on her door, the subsequent whiskies topping up an alcohol level which, at a guess, was pretty constant, at least after closing hours at the optician's. She backed out of the room.

"Don't bother to see me out. I'm really sorry, Pamela. You've had a rotten time of it and James' death has hit you hard. Isn't there someone who could stay with you for a bit? Just till you feel you can cope?"

She grabbed Sylvie's arm. "What did you mean by saying I would never have let you into my home if I'd known the truth?"

Sylvie gently detached the grasping fingers and sidled into the hallway to unlatch the front door, reluctantly turning to confess the bitter secret.

"Adele was my sister."

Twenty-Five

"Hi, Sylvie. It's me, Fiona. I've changed my mind about Ibsen."

"You're coming tomorrow night for the opening? What brought this on?"

"Gary Trenchard. You know, the estate agent, remember? I mentioned that you were getting up a party and as it happens he's got the use of his sister's pad in Maida Vale while she's on holiday. He's driving us both up if that's OK?"

"Great. Ian's coming and my new friend Kevin. I'll leave tickets on the door for you."

"It gets better. Gary wants to treat us all to supper afterwards. He's closed a terrific deal and wants to party. Can you book somewhere for all of us, somewhere that takes late bookings?"

"How many?"

"Make it for six in case your pal Kevin wants to bring a friend. Gary can afford it. Keep your fingers crossed, love, I may even pull it off over the weekend."

"With Gary? I thought you weren't that keen."

"Look, it's only for the weekend, Sylvie. I'm not signing away my beautiful body on a long lease."

Sylvie laughed. "But you could be tempted?"

"Who knows? Anyway, can I leave it with you to fix it? Book it in the name of Trenchard, wait, I'll give you his phone number, these London restaurants get a bit edgy saving a table for six on a Saturday night."

"How about Le Pendu? It's not too pricy and I can guarantee they'll wait till we get there, no need to put Gary's head on the block."

"Will you be able to get away straight after the show?"

"No problem. Frankly I think Harry Garnett finds my evil eye on his new lead a problem. Hey, what do you think? A guy I know at the RSC stopped me as I was leaving the rehearsal rooms one afternoon last week and asked if I'd be interested in an audition."

"At Stratford? Seriously?"

"Yes, seriously. He'd seen my work in New York last year and says he'd like me to try out for the company. Sounds great, doesn't it? Just the break I've been waiting for. But don't mention it in front of the others tonight. Keep your mouth buttoned, my sweet. See you after the show."

Sylvie bounced out of Leslie's office to look for Kevin who was in the kitchen deboning a turkey. She told him the news about Gary Trenchard's offer of dinner for six after the performance.

"Could you book it for me? Warn Terry it'll be after eleven – as soon as we can make it."

"Sure, no problem. Who's coming?"

"Me, you, Fiona, Ian and Gary, of course."

"That's five."

"Well, I thought we'd make it a round number. You could bring one of your mates if you can persuade any of them to sit through the play. Or even join us afterwards if you like. I leave it to you. Help yourself to tickets from the pile on the hallstand. The blokes here are definitely not fighting for ringside seats."

Curtain up went smoothly and the theatre was almost full, mostly freebies Sylvie guessed, Garnett wanting to ensure that the critics he had persuaded to come along would get the right impression. In fairness, the Rep had a good reputation and put on creditable performances, but Harry's insistence on high standards of scripts as well as actors could work against him, the classic repertoire he chose drawing ever fewer punters at a time when competition in fringe theatre was uninhibited.

She peeped from the wings, spying her own little fan club seated together in the stalls, also recognising not only the RSC talent scout sitting with her agent in the front row but, surprise, surprise, an elegantly turned out man sitting with Kevin, their heads close together over the programme as Joanna made her entrance.

Afterwards, she slipped away as quickly as possible, pausing only to respond to her agent's eager congratulations and to mention, sotto voce, her agreement about the Shakespeare audition.

The others were waiting in the foyer, their naked enthusiasm for the show quelling her misgivings about the bloody play. It would get better. Sure to. And Joanna wasn't really that bad, just inexperienced, heady with the thrill of her first success. They made their way to the restaurant jammed into two taxis, Kevin following with his prosperous-looking companion.

Le Pendu was still at full throttle when they arrived although most of the diners were already on to brandy and smokes, the air heady with coffee fumes, wine and the buzz of Saturday night out on the town. Many had, at a guess, tipped out from the National Theatre, Le Pendu enjoying a reputation as an easy-going bistro for late dining.

It was not until they were all seated that they got properly introduced, Kevin having already acquainted everyone else with his new friend. Sylvie was the only one still bemused by Kevin's sly partnership.

"Sylvie, let me introduce you to my friend and colleague, Ray Colthorpe, Le Pendu's wine merchant and a real theatre buff. He loved your performance."

The man stood, politely holding out his hand to kiss her own in the most gallant manner. Terry trundled in with two bottles of champagne to celebrate Sylvie's opening night, delighted to see Colthorpe having such a grand time, delighted to whisper in Gary's ear that Ray was footing the wine bill if that was all right?

All in all it turned out to be one hell of a party, Ian alone being subdued, not drinking at all, excusing his abstinence with, "Sorry folks, I'm driving." Sylvie had no chance of a private word with him but squeezed his knee under the table, anxiously smiling into his drawn features. Poor love's had a bad week, she thought, and probably finds us lot too loud by half. Ray Colthorpe was very jolly, clearly taken with Kevin who had abandoned the wig for the evening and looked very smooth in an open-necked shirt and the new blazer.

"Sylvie, I've got to get back tonight," Ian whispered. "Sorry, sweetheart, but there's been a breakthrough on a series of country house break-ins and I've no option but to get back straight away. Nearly didn't make it at all tonight but I pulled rank, stamped my big copper's feet and I've been let out till morning."

"Oh, Ian! I was banking on our first Sunday lie-in since rehearsals started."

He shrugged, applying himself to the shellfish pasta. "We'll have to talk. Let's pop into the bar for a smoke when they serve coffee. OK? I'll have to leave after that but there's something important to tell you."

The supper party progressed in leaps and bounds, Kevin cheerfully absorbing the witty repartee bouncing across the table which must have seemed a far cry from the banter around Leslie's telly every Saturday night. Sylvie sat on his right and when Ian responded to Fiona's jibe about a policeman's lot not being a happy one, Sylvie took the chance to tell Kevin about her visit to Pamela Ferguson and to assure him that she had confirmed the widow's total exclusion from her ex's business interests. He looked relieved.

"Ray assured me he'll get his own lawyer on to it for

us. He's spoken to Toomey for me. I'm going to see him tomorrow night. I'm borrowing Ray's car."

Sylvie nodded, stealing a glance at the wine merchant who had taken up Kevin's cause, hoping to God he was a good man, Kevin being much too vulnerable for casual treatment at this crossroads in his life.

"I asked her about that child's grave featured in the anonymous letter, Kevin. Adele *was* involved. I've decided to take some flowers to put on Erica's grave after all. Ian can't stay tonight – I'll go tomorrow. It's in a churchyard near Eastbourne, not Norfolk after all. Adele would have wanted me to make some sort of final gesture on her behalf. It's a tragic story. I'll tell you about it when we've got a moment to ourselves."

"Erica you said?"

"Yes. You don't remember the case, surely? It was nine years ago at least."

"No. But it makes sense, don't you see? Erica – heather. It's the Latin name for it. I told you I worked at a garden centre – picked up all sort of tips on that job. One of these days I'll have a garden of my own. Pretty name that, Erica."

"That must have been why Adele got those flowers specially made up," she breathed. "White heather. I'll have to find some somehow even if I have to pinch it from the park on our way home."

The conversation moved on round the table, Terry Barker joining them for a nightcap just as the rest of his clientele made their farewells. He bolted the door and accepted one of Ray's cigars, their heads locked over Le Pendu's current wine list.

Ian and Sylvie slipped into the tiny bar, taking their drinks with then, lighting up their cigarettes and leaning against each other like two trees in the wind.

"There's something I've got to tell you. I got a phone call from Rachel Wilkinson, the inspector in charge of

the Ferguson enquiry, just as I was leaving. Professor
Morrison's walked into the Cambridge nick and given
himself up."

"Given himself up? For what?"

"He's confessed to murdering Ferguson. She's travelling
up there to interview him herself."

"Adele's husband says *he* killed Ferguson? But I thought
he had already been questioned about it."

"And eliminated."

"Is there new evidence?"

"I don't know."

"Will she let you sit in on the interview?"

"No. I can't. I've got my hands full with this other thing,
the robberies. My Super's not interested in the Ferguson
case, and Wilkinson won't want me there."

"But he's innocent."

"More than likely. Barking mad if you ask me but there
you go. He presented himself on a plate, and now has to
go through a thorough rehash of the whole thing."

Sylvie took a drag on her cigarette, frowning fiercely
into the mirror behind the bar.

"Can I visit him?" she said at last.

"I'll see what I can do. I'll ring you at Leslie's tomorrow
night, OK? They'll keep him on ice for as long as possible,
probably need a psychiatric report if he sticks to this barmy
confession."

"He didn't do it, did he? What did he say, for God's
sake?"

"I can't discuss it with you, Sylvie. I'll speak to you
tomorrow night."

The party broke up and piled into taxis, Ian setting off
on his own back to Suffolk, Sylvie clutching Kevin to her
like a lifeline as they were carried back to Leslie's.

"Adele's husband, the professor, has confessed to murdering James Ferguson, Kevin. Just walked into the police
station in Cambridge and gave himself up."

There wasn't much he could say. Clearly Sylvie didn't believe Morrison to be the killer but, in his own mind it made sense. Jealousy was a terrible thing and the bloke had been obsessed with his wife's lover for years, her yearning for younger men poisoning his life. Kevin had talked to Terry about it and Terry thought the Mad Prof, as he called him, had all but got away with it. Kevin held his tongue, letting Sylvie's exhaustion take its toll as her head slipped on to his shoulder and she slept for the rest of the ride home.

In the second taxi, Fiona, high as a kite, clung to Gary Trenchard who seemed to have had, to his own surprise, one hell of a good time.

Twenty-Six

S ylvie woke late, her head banging like a door caught in the wind. She groaned, turned over and, suffocating her hangover under the pillow, resolved to get back to sleep. Leslie's boarders were clearly still lost to the world, not a sound from anywhere as later she tottered down to the basement kitchen to brew some strong coffee. Not even Kevin was up and about on this gloomy Sunday morning and, as she climbed back up the thinly carpeted stairs, it occurred to her that having given Leslie notice, he was wisely keeping his head down.

The caffeine dealt the raw spots a knock-out at last and she decided to drive round to see if she could find a shop or a flower barrow which could make up a heather bouquet for Erica's grave. Driving down to Sussex would fill an empty day, searching the Bonningstone churchyard for an Erica who had died nine or ten years ago an intriguing puzzle. Ian was incommunicado – his cell phone was switched off and a call she made to his office met with a blunt response.

"The inspector's interviewing a suspect," the sergeant informed her, refusing to take a personal message, unimpressed by Sylvie's velvet tones.

She toured the district, even confronting the bloke manning the flower stall outside a cemetery.

"White heather? No call for it, love. By the time people get dug in here," he said, cocking a thumb at the cemetery gates, "their luck's already run out."

"It's for a young girl. Isn't there anywhere I can get it?"

He grimaced. "Nine Elms would do you if you're up there early – got every bloody flower there but they get packed up by nine."

"Nine Elms? Where's that?"

"Flower market out Battersea way. Can't miss it and you can park there, no problem."

"I need the heather today."

"Sorry, love, can't help you." He shrugged, wrapping a bunch of yellow chrysanthemums for an old woman dressed in black.

Sylvie sat in her car wondering what to do next. Laying flowers on the child's grave was a final gesture she felt she owed Adele, a belated offering her sister had intended to take down to Sussex after her weekend with Underwood at Swan House. But another idea surfaced, even more tempting than the mawkish completion of her private vow regarding the bunch of heather. Fired up with this new anxiety, Sylvie drove back to Leslie's and ran upstairs to use the pay phone on the landing.

Getting the number from Directory Enquiries for Inspector Rachel Wilkinson's temporary headquarters in Cambridge was easy, persuading the officer on duty to allow her to speak to the woman herself took a whole lot of backchat, Sylvie this time choosing to take an aggressive stance, refusing to be fobbed off as she had been when trying to speak to Ian at his police station.

"This is Professor Morrison's sister-in-law speaking. His only relative. I am utterly appalled that he is being held when clearly the man's medical condition is in question. I demand to see my brother-in-law at once," she spat, repeating her name with full dramatic force.

After a further delay, her coins rattling into Leslie's pay phone like it was a one-armed bandit, the elusive Inspector Wilkinson, Ian's bête noire, came on the line.

Her tone was cool, her reception of Sylvie's remonstrations guarded. But in the face of Sylvie's genuine reservations about Laurence Morrison's state of mind, it was agreed that she might see him that afternoon and reassure herself that the self-confessed killer of James Ferguson was indeed in a fit mental state to be kept under lock and key until a decision had been made about the charge.

Sylvie dressed with care, changing into a black trouser suit and suede boots, knotting her long hair into a chignon, looking faintly Spanish and certainly no pushover. She wondered how the professor would accept this dark angel claiming to be his next-of-kin, and seriously doubted whether his feelings for Adele would soften his attitude to the sister who seemed determined to scotch this suicidal desire to lay his head on the block. Unless he could produce new evidence supporting his confession, Sylvie could never see that the man's story would hold up, his movements on the night in question having already, according to Ian, been exposed to Rachel Wilkinson's fierce interrogation, quite apart from her only witness refusing to pick out Morrison on the identity parade.

She arrived in Cambridge shortly after one o'clock and had a bite to eat and a glass of wine in a pub down by the river, the falling leaves from the willows swirling in the air to settle on the water like paper fishes.

Her appointment was at two and, on the dot, she presented herself at the sergeant's desk and, after a brief telephone conversation, was led along the corridor and down some steps into the basement. Morrison was seated in an interview room, the door unlocked but with a constable standing to one side. Sylvie wished she had brought something with her though, on reflection, what would be an appropriate offering for a man determined to make a martyr of himself?

Laurence Morrison did not look like a martyr. Quite the

reverse, astonishingly chipper in fact. Sylvie felt her sympathies seeping away, the man's insufferable ego stiffening his very posture, a sarcastic smile on his lips as she slid on to the chair opposite him at the wide table. She did not smile and made no attempt to stretch out a hand to greet him.

"Why are you here?" he barked. "I tried to refuse to see you but I seem to have no authority in this benighted place."

"What the hell do you expect? You'll be lucky to escape without a charge of wasting police time, Larry."

"Hardly the kind words of 'my only living relative' as I understand you described yourself to the inspector," he said with undisguised irony. "Perhaps we should introduce ourselves. You certainly bear no resemblance to my late wife but I do know your face, of course, from photographs at the cottage. I live there now, you know, my rooms in college having been withdrawn. Officially, I am on sabbatical leave but once the ballyhoo has died down my formal resignation will be announced. A fit conclusion to a rather spotted academic career, do you not agree?"

"Cut the crap, Larry, and let's get down to business. What's the game? Why confess to killing Ferguson? Either you're barking mad or your twisted notion of retribution has gone right off the Richter scale."

"Have you a cigarette? I seem to have mislaid mine."

She fumbled in her bag and produced some smokes and a match folder, the constable at her elbow nodding in response to her "OK?"

Morrison took a drag on the cigarette, his eyes boring into Sylvie's, their antagonism softening as the pause in the mental conflict grew into a full two minutes' silence. To rattle his cage she produced the anonymous letter from her wallet, and smoothed it out on the table.

"Why did you send this?" she demanded, pushing the cigarette pack out of reach.

He started to protest, blustering denials, but having been caught off balance his confidence was sorely dented. She interrupted, cutting short the flurried rebuttal.

"Look, I haven't driven all this way to listen to a pack of lies, Larry. Believe it or not, I'm here to help you, God knows why."

He inhaled deeply, the scraggy sinews in his neck jerking like twine. He was tieless, probably also without belt and shoelaces she guessed, the psychiatric assessment of this highly intelligent nutter being still under review. Sylvie's uncompromising stance paid off and as he stubbed out the butt in the tin ashtray, she pushed the pack across the table, like a carrot for a bloody donkey she reflected. He lit a second cigarette and after an initial drag, started to speak.

"Did you visit the grave?"

"Not yet."

His mouth puckered petulantly. "That was the whole point, you stupid woman. To make you see what she had done. Adele was not the saintly figure she pretended to be. She never told you, did she, about that child's death, the fact that her disgusting affair with Ferguson directly resulted in his dereliction of duty? That poor child should have been given their full attention – they were *in loco parentis*. Unforgivable behaviour. Adele didn't care a jot for anyone, you know. Left Ferguson to take the blame, made no apology to me for the enormous anguish I suffered, not to mention the snide innuendos to which I was exposed from the college fraternity. My career suffered because of your sister. This ultimate sad pass I am now in can be directly traced back to her casual attitude to everyone, every responsibility. I wanted *you* to know, wanted her sister, the only person to whom Adele wished to stand in good odour, to realise her perfidy. I loved her despite her cruelty. I knew her for what she was and now she's dead I've nothing to live for. But I wanted *you* to know the facts."

"But the child's death was so long ago, Larry, why flagellate yourself with old guilt on her behalf? It was utterly reprehensible I agree, but when Erica died, Adele was young – and having a dangerous affair under the eyes of the rest of the staff at that stuffy school would have seemed exciting. No-one, least of all Adele, could have guessed the consequences of their cavalier treatment of the children in their charge. They were teenagers, after all, not infants. The girl who died had habitually fallen behind the rest of the school party, she was even suspected of pushing off back to England on her own. The tragedy was the result of a terrible juxtaposition of circumstances but Adele *did* care. She bought flowers to put on Erica's grave the very weekend she herself died. It all happened years and years ago, Larry. It was over long ago."

He smiled grimly. "No, it's not. It's not over yet. Did you discover her name?"

"Erica?"

"Erica Toomey."

"Toomey?"

"She was the only child of the man Ferguson was trying to squeeze money out of. I confronted Ferguson about it. I saw them together at the restaurant and recognised the child's father immediately, he's hardly changed. I berated Ferguson, thought at first he might not have realised the connection but he knew all right. As brass-necked as that wife of mine, he had no conscience about being one of the causes of the girl's death and then was even taking a begging bowl to her grieving parents."

"Why should Toomey get involved?"

"I tackled Ferguson about that. Mr Toomey was intro-duced by someone in the wine trade. Ferguson's a common enough name and at first he was an innocent dupe. The years had taken their toll, Ferguson was no longer the handsome lover Adele flaunted. He had lost everything in the fallout from the murder in France, including his looks. Mr Toomey hadn't changed that much, he was older to start with, of course, but his years in prison had barely touched him it seemed to me. He must be the forgiving type, maybe he came to God while he was serving his sentence – so many of them do I'm told."

"You've spoken to Toomey?"

"No, never. But I dogged Ferguson's every move, all my hatred of the barefaced affrontery of the man curdling the old bitterness. I could not forgive. How dare he beg Mr Toomey for money after what had happened?"

"The man had to make a living, Larry. If he managed to patch things up with the girl's father that was all to the good. Even old wounds heal and yours would too if you gave them a chance. Why throw yourself in the lion's den now, claiming responsibility for a random street killing which has been shown to be the work of an overenthusiastic mugger?"

"Ferguson was a liar and a manipulator just like her. But he did admit to me that he had explained to Mr Toomey that the blame was Adele's. She had been warned that Erica was unhappy and wanted to fly home and Matron expressly directed your sister to pay particular attention to the child, the girls being Adele's special responsibility as the only female member of staff actually cycling along with the school party. Mr Toomey accepted all this from Ferguson and agreed to get financially involved with Le Pendu but then he found out that Ferguson had lied, was still involved with Adele, probably still conducting an affair with my wife. This upset Mr Toomey or so Ferguson told me though he didn't pull out of his investment until later it seems."

"That wasn't the full truth, Larry. Adele and Jimmy Ferguson were not lovers. You've got it all wrong. He found out Adele had made a lot of money and only contacted her as a back-up in case Toomey changed his mind. It was a business deal. Adele was hoping to marry somene else, a book dealer called Underwood."

Morrison wiped the sweat from his upper lip, his hand trembling.

"Adele could never remarry. She was my wife."

Sylvie sighed. "We're not getting anywhere with this, are we? You still can't explain why you say you attacked Ferguson on the bridge."

He closed his eyes, his extreme pallor giving her serious cause for alarm. She glanced at the constable who frowned but made no move to cut short the visit. It occurred to Sylvie that her meeting with Morrison might be bugged to back up the constable's evidence. The sly inspector, Rachel Wilkinson, probably hoped that Morrison's sister-in-law would prise more than a bald admission of guilt from the professor. But that couldn't happen in England, could it? All that sort of undercover surveillance only happened in crime stuff churned out on TV, surely.

He spoke again, his voice harsh. "I needed to kill him, don't you see? He killed me years ago. In my mind I struck him over and over again, night after night, hating that man more each day what with his indefatigable pursuit of my wife. She was asking for a divorce. They thought they could divert me with that Underwood fellow who evaded my efforts to see him. But I'm no fool: Underwood was a blind, merely a client. Adele secretly intended to marry *Ferguson* if she got her divorce. She said I couldn't stop it anyway after our long separation so I pretended to concede but it would never have gone through. Never. If that drifter on the bridge did my work for me, he was merely an instrument of my desires. I *wanted* to kill Ferguson. If I had had the strength and the opportunity, as that mugger did, I would have thrown the devil over the side with glorious elation. I *am* guilty.

I claim his dead body as *my* prize. And then," he added enigmatically, "the true killer will come forward and give himself up."

He slumped in the chair exhausted, his head lolling.

Sylvie rose, knowing there was nothing more to be said, the poor devil had clearly lost his marbles since Adele's death. "I'll come back for you when they let you go, Larry. I'll take you home. You'll be out of here soon."

She walked away, leaving a message for Inspector Wilkinson who was in conference it was claimed, that she would return for her brother-in-law as soon as he was released. They could either hold him for another night or a little longer if an extension of questioning was permitted, or let him go. In the meantime his solicitor would attend she crisply informed the sergeant, jotting down Fiona's home and office telephone numbers on a police memo pad and leaving a call-back number for herself for the next twenty-four hours at the Garden House Hotel.

She was lucky to get a room, the place seething with excitable parents who had dropped off their fledglings for the first taste of university life. She settled in her lovely room and sent down for some sandwiches and a bottle of wine, excusing her need for a decent place to stay on the rigours of juggling a new stage role with the unasked for guardian angel spot for her sister's husband, a man she had always disliked and whose reasons for making such a wild confession were far from clear. Morrison had an ulterior motive she was sure of it but he was balancing on a tightrope, had already ruined his career with this crazy affectation of guilt and now exposed himself to possible psychiatric care at the very least.

Ian was still out of range but luckily Fiona was back from her night out with Gary, the weekend at his sister's flat in Maida Vale having palled like an arranged marriage.

"Nobody told me he's gay!" she wailed. Sylvie agreed to meet Fiona for tea downstairs in an hour.

Poor Fiona. Unlucky in love. Poor me too, she reflected, gazing out at the leaden sky.

Twenty-Seven

S ylvie phoned Leslie's several times before the call was
finally answered by one of the boarders.

"Leslie's having a bit of a kip. Any message, Sylvie?"

"It was really Kevin I wanted to speak to, Charlie. Is he
about?"

"Went out straight after he washed up. Sunday afternoon's he's generally at the shop doing his forecasts."

"Oh, yes, I forgot. You haven't got the number by any
chance? He usually leaves a stack of his cards in the kitchen
behind the clock."

"Half a mo, duck." The faint beat of Radio One crackled
in the background as Charlie shuffled off and when Sylvie
eventually got through to Kevin it was only after she had
let the phone go on ringing for nearly five minutes.

"Oh, Kevin, thank goodness you're still there. I've been
trying to reach you. It's Sylvie. I'm in Cambridge." She
explained about Morrison being detained for questioning
about the Ferguson murder.

"I saw it in the paper. Guessed it was your sister's ex."

"He's been named in the Sunday papers?" Sylvie
exclaimed.

"Well, not named – just said that a Cambridge don had
admitted to the killing of his late wife's lover and the
case is being investigated by a woman detective, I forget
her name. Knew who it was straight off. Even without
a photograph there can't be many of his sort to fit the
bill. Poor old sod must have suffered terrible remorse, his

mind still in ribbons after Adele's death. Do you think he did it?"

"No, I don't. But he's got himself in one hell of a situation and all of his own making. I don't even think he's really mad, Kevin, just a cunning bugger with some sort of agenda of his own. I went to see him this afternoon and I'll take him home later. I hadn't bargained for the press getting hold of the story so soon though, might have to whisk him out through the back door. There's no new evidence as far as I know, just his confession – they'll have to let him go."

"What does Ian say?"

"I can't reach him. Incidentally, are you still planning to visit Toomey at his home tonight?"

"Yeah. About eight he said."

"That's why I had to talk to you. I've found out some more background information about him you should know."

Kevin's heavy sigh hissed along the line like static. "Don't go on about his prison record, Sylv. I've heard it all before. Ray Colthorpe – you remember him from last night? – well, Ray says he's a smashing guy and a good friend of his. I *need* a wine buff on the team, Sylvie, and Toomey would be ideal, especially if he decided to invest in Le Pendu after all and . . ."

Sylvie butted in, clearly anxious. "Did Ray tell you about Toomey's daughter being murdered?"

"Blimey, no! When did this happen?"

"Oh, years ago in France but . . ."

"So what?"

"Just listen, will you? The girl died because Ferguson and my sister failed to take care of her on a school trip. She was only fifteen. My brother-in-law, Larry, says Toomey didn't connect Jimmy Ferguson with this at first but found out later."

"So that was really why he pulled out."

"No. Apparently not. Toomey only changed his mind about Le Pendu after Ferguson died. While negotiations were going on Ferguson must have persuaded Toomey that my sister was really to blame and Toomey, bless his heart, decided to bury the hatchet and forgive Ferguson for his part in the way his girl got lost."

"Lost? I thought you said murdered."

"She was left behind on a cycle ride and a nutcase attacked her. A terrible thing. It's the girl the anonymous letter was all about, the one Adele had that bunch of heather made up for, the flowers I told you about that were found in her hotel room – I think she was going to place them on the grave herself after the weekend. It was an appalling murder, years ago now, of course, but it made headlines in all the British papers at the time they tell me."

"I bet it did! Whew. Thanks for putting me in the picture, Sylvie. I could have put my foot in it with Toomey thinking his criminal record was the only skeleton in the cupboard."

"Just be careful what you say. He forgave Jimmy Ferguson so he must be a decent soul, and if he wants to dip a toe in the restaurant trade Ferguson being out of the way means you all start with a clean sheet."

Kevin laughed. "Don't mince words do you, miss? Bet you're a Capricorn."

"Wrong."

"Look, I've got to get back to work. I'm all behind with my postal forecasts and it'll take a while to drive down to Sussex."

"Sussex?"

"Toomey's place."

"Ah, that probably explains it. His daughter was buried somewhere there. I was going to take some flowers to put on her grave this morning but seeing Larry Morrison spiked my guns."

"When will you be back?"

"Tomorrow afternoon at the latest. I've got a performance in the evening remember."

"Oh yeah. That bossy woman Hedda shoots herself *every* night?"

Sylvie giggled. "Bye Kevin. See you tomorrow. Ring me at the Garden House Hotel in Cambridge if you get a definite answer from Toomey tonight. Good luck!"

She put down the phone and glanced at her watch. It was already time to go down and order tea. She needed to bag a quiet corner where she could give Fiona the lowdown about Larry's confession. She had probably seen the newsflash in the Sunday papers herself and guessed that it was Adele's bloody professor who had put himself in the frame for Ferguson's murder.

Kevin pressed his flannels and brushed the new blazer, the nearest he owned to formal gear. He gazed at his sober reflection in the mirror and decided, on balance, to wear the wig. Since going for broke with Terry Barker, sheltering behind the wigs and turbans he had lived with for so long had suddenly seemed superfluous. Ray Colthorpe readily accepted his bald pate at last night's party without so much as a blink.

But he was nervous. Appealing to Toomey to change his mind was a big deal and the ponytail wig gave him that little extra bit of confidence. If Toomey took up the offer on Le Pendu and the three of them became partners, Kevin promised himself the wigs, together with all Madame Vanda's stuff, would go in the bin. He would continue with the postal readings but Madame Vanda and the cabaret act were a part of his life that was over.

Colthorpe's car, a big blue BMW, was parked outside the shop and Kevin had promised to drive back to Ray's place straight from Sussex to tell him how things had gone.

It was almost dark by the time he got down to the coast, the tide well up, the rhythmic sound of waves breaking on the beach below Toomey's house beating in time with his heart.

The house was a low clifftop building obscured by trees flanking the old coast road. The driveway curved ahead, his headlights cutting a swathe through the dark tunnel of pines. The windows were all lit up and uncurtained, the front door brightly illuminated by security spotlights which flashed on as the car approached. Kevin gathered his briefcase, checked his wig and locked Ray's car, the small intake of breath as he waited for Toomey to answer the doorbell his final gesture of anxiety before he strode into the house.

Twenty-Eight

K evin knew even before he had crossed the threshold that he was going to get nowhere with Alan Toomey that night. The man was clearly drunk.

Swaying slightly as he held out an affable hand to his visitor, Toomey's heavy frame filled the doorway and, as Kevin introduced himself, an undeniable whiff of brandy on the man's breath was confirmed by the bottles and dirty glasses littering the low marble table in the centre of the living room.

"My housekeeper's night off – Sundays," he apologised. "Excuse the mess."

The place was low ceilinged, shaded lamps casting pools of light on to the rugs, modern leather sofas sharply angular. In fact, Kevin had to admit as he sunk into the squeaky cushions, the sofa was enormously comfortable.

Toomey himself lumbered about fixing a gin and tonic for his guest, prattling away about the view which at this late hour was too dark to see. Nevertheless, he insisted in a boozy way on opening the french doors leading on to a terrace cantilevered against the cliff face, the wide paved area thrown into focus with garden spotlights.

Kevin took a deep breath of sea air, the sound of the waves below barely a murmur on this unseasonably warm evening. They moved back inside leaving the doors ajar, the net curtain billowing into the room like a spinnaker. It was overheated and underfurnished, the two man-size sofas flanking the coffee table augmented only by a single metal-framed console table bearing bottles and glasses and little else. There were no photographs and no books, the sole decoration being a bowl of fresh heather blooming in shades of purple and mauve.

Toomey wore trainers, a stained tee shirt and jeans, his powerful shoulders drooping under the thin fabric, his fingers toying nervously with the glass in his hand. Kevin got straight to the point, guessing that the attention span of his melancholic host was low. He described the proposals for Le Pendu, fanning out the new business plans on the table and passing over the wine list which Ray Colthorpe had amended.

Toomey stared without animation, his eyes vacant as he paid lip service to Kevin's eager forecasts. Then, without warning, he jumped up, refilled his balloon glass and moved to the open door to gaze out at the barely visible horizon, his back to Kevin whose delivery stuttered and finally ceased.

"I'm not coming in with you, lad. You realise that, don't you?"

"Won't you give it further thought, Mr Toomey? I would be happy to leave these proposals for you to study later. Mr Colthorpe is enthusiastic about the future of Le Pendu and hoped to interest you – only as a business sideline, of course and . . ."

"I don't care a fuck about Le Pendu," he said, turning to face him with a chilly smile. Kevin sighed, shuffling the papers together with resignation.

"Is it because of Ferguson? Because if you're worried you needn't be. The police will close the investigation very soon, they already have a suspect in custody. You won't be drawn into any publicity yourself, Mr Toomey."

"You're talking about that prat Morrison I suppose. Adele's professor? I read about his phony confession in the papers this morning. Is the man totally mad?"

He slumped on to the sofa, boneless as a sack.

"I believe so, sir. It's not official but my friend Sylvie has been to see Morrison at the police station."

"Sylvie? Adele's sister? Yes, she's the sort who would," he retorted, his red-rimmed eyes sparking with anger.

"You know her?"

"Sylvie? No, but I knew her sister extremely well. As unlike as two sisters could be, I understand, in temperament as well as looks."

"You knew Adele? I suppose Ferguson introduced you."

"No. I had been 'intimate' as they say with that young lady for some time. She puts herself about that one."

Kevin's eyes widened. "She died you realise."

"Not before time."

The man heaved himself out of the seat, breathing laboriously, apparently mesmerised by the flowers on the coffee table. He looked across at his guest, suddenly all smiles, his rapid mood swings prompting in Kevin serious doubts about the volatile situation he found himself in.

"I love heather, don't you? Here, boy, put this in your buttonhole. For luck." He swiftly broke off a sprig and dropped it in his lap. Kevin delicately took up the sprig of heather and laid it in the palm of his hand, deciding, on balance, that Toomey was too inebriated to be a real cause of trouble. He'd seen drunks like him before at the club: great louts boozed to the eyeballs, shouting their heads off. And he'd seen them heaved outside by Kelly's henchmen like so much flotsam to sprawl in the gutter, their weight and strength tottering at a touch.

"Sylvie told me about your daughter, Mr Toomey. Erica. It must have broken your heart."

Angry tears welled up as he muttered, "They killed her you know, between them they did for my little girl while they looked the other way, leaving the poor kid to grapple with that French farmhand all alone. What chance did she have?"

"But you forgave him, didn't you? Forgave Ferguson. It wasn't his fault."

"He blamed Adele and she blamed him. A right couple of liars the pair of them. It destroyed my wife, of course."

"What?"

"Didn't Ray tell you the rest of it? I was already banged up for that bloody wine fraud and my stupid wife sent Erica off to France to slim her down she said. That was the sort of woman she was – forever on a diet herself and making my daughter utterly miserable with her criticism. Only made Erica worse, of course. Eating disorders aren't just starvation binges, you know. Unhappiness can make people fat. Fat and jolly so they say, but it isn't like that for girls like my Erica. The more Joyce nagged her about her weight the more depressed she became."

He swigged the brandy down like a draught of medication.

"Not that I don't blame myself, Kevin. I was in prison and it's possible her friends teased her about her Dad being inside. I was in no position to take Erica's part and when that stinking pervert murdered her, I blamed Joyce. Hit out blindly in all directions and some poor warder caught it. I broke his jaw when he made a snide remark. Governor told me that her body was being flown back to the school grounds in a private plane and buried quietly in the local churchyard. But because I had attacked the bloody screw I was considered too vicious to be allowed out they said. Buggered up my early release on top of it – a moment's burst of frustration had sealed me up for extra time. I bet Joyce told them I'd threatened to get even with her over her miserable treatment of the poor kid. Too dangerous to be allowed out! Can you believe it? My only child flown back in a coffin and me not allowed home leave? That finished Joyce. She couldn't hack it on her own. She hanged herself from the bannisters two weeks after the funeral, too scared to face me, knowing as soon as they let me out I'd be round to get her, put her head in a vice for sending my darling girl away, refusing to listen to her cry for help."

He threw his glass into the hearth where it shattered into a hundred pieces and strolled on to the terrace.

Kevin leapt up, crushing the flowers in his fist, his mind's eye filling with blood as clearly as the visions he saw in the tarot cards. Suddenly everything fell into place, Ferguson's plunge into the river a murderous replay of the drowning of the little girl in France. He rushed out after him on to the terrace, appalled at the man's revenge distilled in years of detailed planning.

"You gave Ferguson a sprig of heather before he died, didn't you, Toomey?" he said, gripping the man's shoulder in barely suppressed rage.

Toomey leaned over the railing staring down at the breakers on the rocks below, Kevin behind him like a shadow.

"How did you arrange for someone to kill him?"

Toomey's bitter laughter caught in the wind off the sea. "Pay someone else? Why would I do that? It was very simple. I just pushed him over the edge."

"That's impossible. He was there alone. You had already left the Savoy in a taxi, the doorman saw you."

"The cab dropped me at the other end of the bridge. I knew Ferguson would have to pass that way on his route home. I waited and walked towards him when I saw that lying creep striding along the walkway. He was surprised to see me."

"But the witness told the police the man he saw was a fan wearing a supporter's scarf, the killer was some sort of soccer hooligan."

He shrugged. "Takes just one eye-catcher to throw a half-cut witness off track. It was dark. A scarf and baseball cap in a carrier bag, stash the jacket and tie – you don't need a balaclava to disguise yourself. All those years banged up with clever villains taught me a thing or two and I had plenty of time to work it out. How does that stupid professor tell it?"

"He confessed. Claims he killed Ferguson himself. In revenge."

Toomey's laugh broke on a bitter note and he grabbed Kevin's lapels.

"He had no bloody right. Ferguson was *my* victim. Morrison had no right I tell you! Faking a confession, pretending he was man enough to claim retribution. Retribution for what? For his wife being a whore who jumped into bed with any man willing to pay? Mine was the only true vengeance and I had years and years in a cell to brew my hatred, to plan how I would kill them both, drown them just as my poor sweet baby was drowned, make them realise at the end they had not escaped me after all."

"Ferguson *and* Adele? You drowned Adele? You bloody liar! You weren't even there, Toomey. You're as bad as Morrison, both of you fighting over a corpse like a pair of hyenas," he said with a explosion of anger.

"Oh, yeah! Who says I wasn't there when that hooker snuffed it? Who do you think staged that fucking fight in the hotel room knowing the old busybody in the next room would hear every word? Who was seen to drive away? Who do you think Underwood is and why do you think he would help me?"

"Underwood? *Underwood* was your accomplice!"

Toomey smiled. "It was easy to get Adele on her mobile a little later, to ring from a callbox, beg forgiveness for my bout of temper, propose a romantic reconciliation, say I'd join the silly bitch in the pool for a last private skinny dip before we left next morning. We'd frolicked there before like a couple of seals, any chance we got – always at night when the rest of them were asleep. I strolled straight in through the patio doors. We larked about in the dark but quietly, careful not to make any disturbance which would bring that garden boy nosing round again. Pulling her under the water by her hair till she stopped breathing was child's play."

"And you just walked away?"

"Dried myself off on a towel from the changing room, put on my clothes and slipped out through the garden the way I'd come. Then I crept up the fire escape and let myself into our room. I needed to snatch her laptop and her mobile phone. She kept notes about clients on her computer and I had to make sure she hadn't mentioned Toomey. She already suspected Underwood was not my real name and I had to be certain there was nothing in her diary or in the personal snippets she recorded about her clients which made the slightest connection. She was a bright girl, Adele. And I'd tested her as much as I dare with questions about her affair with Ferguson."

"Why the phone?"

"I was worried about the calls she might have made. That silly bugger, Morrison, was making a nuisance of himself – as Underwood I had my work cut out keeping out of his way! I wasn't sure if the phone records would lead the police to question him – he used to dog her every move if he could. The last thing I wanted was for the mobile to fall into the wrong hands, recording Morrison's stupid messages perhaps."

"What did you do with it?"

"I threw it into the sea."

"And the computer?"

"Destroyed. All wasted effort as it happens. That stupid bint had not quite realised that Underwood and Toomey were one and the same – Erica's father – the poor grieving bastard who couldn't even kiss his daughter's coffin before it got grassed over."

Toomey spoke quite evenly. Kevin, entirely rivetted by the awful truth felt his anger rising, forgetting to be afraid of a man convicted of uncontrollable violence.

His voice rumbled on. "It was only later I found the

key for room number sixteen in the car, realised I'd left the other one on reception with my tips. Slipping the key into Ferguson's pocket as we talked on the footbridge was a melodramatic touch. I wanted to make the police sit up and take notice. I didn't realise he had press cuttings about Adele's death in his pocket. He told me he had finished with her but he lied to me. Sliding the hotel key in his jacket was egging the pudding. Stupid of me. Just goes to show you should always stick to the plan – never embellish a perfect crime with last minute frills."

"And nobody linked you with Underwood?"

"Why should they? The book business was an inheritance from my wife. I changed the name and traded under it – it was useful having a dual identity. Having successfully orchestrated a major fraud which all but ruined the wine trade, constructing a convenient alter ego was no problem at all. Choosing the name Brendon was an ironic allusion to my 'place of rehabilitation' as they are keen to dub it. Grendon is the location of a prison near Aylesbury where they have voluntary group therapy sessions for the inmates. It's supposed to make them come to terms with their anger," he said with a snort of derision. "Being trapped in those cells for so many years merely gave me the time to form a plan, solidified my resolve to kill them both. Two deaths for the deaths of my wife and my child which were both attributable to Adele Morrison and Jimmy Ferguson."

"What now?" Kevin demanded. "Will you give yourself up so they can release the professor?"

"Why should I? That stupid man dug a hole for himself, he can dig himself out. He wanted to claim the 'honour' of killing Ferguson which made me angry at first but in the long run why get worked up about it? Let Morrison set himself up as an instrument of justice if that's what turns him on. I shall be free at last. I shall be free to put ten years of bitterness behind me, to lay a bouquet of heather on Erica's grave and get on with the rest of my life."

"*You* bought the heather they found at the hotel? Sylvie thought Adele intended to put those flowers on your daughter's grave. She thought her sister still remembered Erica each year on the anniversary of her death."

He moved in on Kevin, his eyes narrowed. "Adele buy flowers for Erica's grave? Have you still no idea what kind of a woman she was? Adele had never given my child a single moment's thought in years. I bought the flowers as a test but it meant nothing to Adele – even when, as Underwood, I teased her about her affair with the schoolmaster in France, said I'd read about it in the papers at the time, recognised her straight away when she introduced herself as a property finder. It took me a year to track her down after I was released – and *she* thought she was the clever one! That bitch was as caring as a rabid dog, she'd even forgotten Erica's surname."

"You can't just leave it like that! Leave poor bloody Morrison to take the rap."

"To claim the kudos you mean?" he acidly retorted. "No, I thought when I read the papers this morning that Morrison jumping in to claim *my* revenge would be too much. But, on reflection, so what? Let him fry. Let that sanctimonious bugger find out what it's like being banged up like an animal."

"I shall have to tell Sylvie the truth," Kevin countered. "She deserves that much."

Toomey spun round, instantly sober, recognising the awesome light of determination in the boy's eyes. He was upon him in a flash, grabbing Kevin by the throat and forcing him hard against the railings. The sea churned below, the tide ebbing from the stony beach, the sound of the shingle rhythmic in the darkness.

They fought for what seemed to Kevin minutes but in one last desperate throw he hooked a foot around Toomey's ankle and his opponent momentarily released his grip. Kevin swung round but it was too late, Toomey grabbed his hair but the wig came away in his hand, taking him by surprise. They lurched against the railing spinning together like dancers, the heavier man smashing his victim against the rusty ironwork again and again.

There was a loud crack as part of the railing broke away and both men faltered, holding on to each other as their balance shifted and then, as the rest of the metal section buckled and then came clear away from its housing, Toomey crashed over the edge pulling Kevin with him into the void, their cries unheard, the ebbing tide drowning their screams.

Twenty-Nine

S unday night was a time of frustration all round. Ray Colthorpe didn't get his car back, Ian could not track down Sylvie at the boarding house and Sylvie, hearing nothing from Kevin at her hotel that evening, concluded his appeal to Toomey to come in on the restaurant deal had fallen on deaf ears and that he had been too dispirited to ring her.

It was not until Monday morning when Toomey's housekeeper arrived back on duty and discovered the broken railings on the terrace and spied two bodies spreadeagled on the beach below that the alarm was raised. By the time the emergency services had manoeuvred lifting gear to winch up the broken bodies, the poor woman was utterly distraught.

She failed to recognise the younger man but, despite the awesome facial injuries Toomey had sustained, Mrs Brightwell tearfully identified her employer. The visitor's car belonged to a Mr Colthorpe the police ascertained but when he nervously responded to their call and confirmed ownership it was still several minutes before his garbled explanation regarding the loan of the vehicle and the name of its driver cleared the confusion.

"Your friend is in intensive care, Mr Colthorpe, but the other gentleman died on impact. A terrible accident but we think—"

"Which friend?" Colthorpe interrupted, his voice ragged with anxiety.

"The younger man is the one in hospital, sir. Mr Last I think you said. Perhaps you would be good enough to come down and collect your car."

"May I see Mr Last?"

"He's unconscious, of course, and visiting would be at the discretion of the surgeon. There were several serious injuries including a cracked skull but the operation went smoothly. Are you family?"

"There is no family. I'll come down straight away, I know the house. Mr Toomey was also a friend of mine."

It was only later on the train that Colthorpe thought to ring Le Pendu and break the news to Terry Barker.

"Jesus Christ, Ray! Both backers dead. I'll have to close down now."

"Kevin survived. Why don't you join me, Terry? The restaurant's closed on Mondays, isn't it?"

They agreed to meet at the house so Ray could use his car and Terry packed an overnight bag just in case. He had been right all along – they should have changed the name long ago. First Ferguson and now Toomey and Kevin. The place was definitely jinxed. When, on the journey down, his thoughts had had a chance to settle, it crossed his mind that if Kevin recovered and was still game to carry on at Le Pendu, Ray Colthorpe might be persuaded to take up the third share in the business. He could afford it and the suspicion had always lurked at the back of his mind that the old bloke was gay. Never had a boyfriend as far as he knew but hope, fanned by a genuine affection for both of them, made such an unlikely pairing seem worth a bet.

Colthorpe joined him in the hospital canteen after he had parked the car, the two of them anxiously waiting for good news. The initial police assessment of the accident was that the rusty ironwork had been corroded for some time, the erosion caused by bad maintenance and salt spray causing metal fatigue which an owner attentive to the safety rail should have spotted. Kevin was still unconscious, his fall having been broken by Toomey's own body, a macabre fact which was not lost on Sylvie when she heard the details.

Sylvie was unable to leave London, her loyalty to Garnett's Rep taking precedence over any anxiety about poor Kevin who had, as was clearly evident, been snatched from the jaws of death and now sported two guardian angels at the bedside.

Sylvie had a theory about the worry factor. Sylvie's theory was that everyone had a level of anxiety which remained constant whatever the circumstances. If one had a huge problem to cope with, the worry factor entirely filled the vacuum and, if not, minor problems would ratchet up to maintain the same level personal to each according to his or her temperament. This idea was utterly unscientific and only sustained by her own powers of observation but it was an interesting way of containing the slings and arrows of outrageous fortune.

In her own case, worrying about Morrison was of paramount importance and working herself up about Kevin Last could only be slotted in when, at midday on the Monday, she received an urgent call from Fiona to say she had negotiated his release.

"There wasn't a bit of proof you know, Sylvie. That snotty female, Inspector Wilkinson, has already driven back to London, glad to get away from provincial time wasters like Larry Morrison and who can blame her? Could you be a darling and take him off my hands? I've got to get back to the office for a meeting."

Sylvie drove her silent passenger home to Adele's cottage outside the city, his face grey with fatigue, the poor devil evidently chastened by his night in custody. The opinion of the psychiatrist called in to question his ability to be interviewed had been equivocal, finding himself curiously wrong-footed when the man suddenly withdrew his confession, pulled himself together and apologised with a sad smile for his inexplicable "mental blackout" as he called it. On balance the shrink decided Morrison was no more looney than the average university don.

The sergeant who accompanied Sylvie and Morrison to her car was as mystified as everyone else. Being a local man with an inbuilt reverence for "them clever academics" as he called them, he had been worried by Morrison's extraordinary desire to blame himself for a murder which even the woman detective, brought specially from London to question him, had scant reason to take seriously. He pulled Sylvie aside out of earshot.

"These professors overcook their brains if you ask me," he confided as they waited for Morrison fussily to settle himself in the front seat. "I let him borrow my little radio after he refused his breakfast, thought a bit of nice music would take his mind off his troubles. We get people coming in with false confessions all the time, miss. Can't think what excitement they get out of it."

"Lending your radio was very kind of you but I don't think my brother-in-law's much of a music fan, sergeant. More of a reader really."

"You're right there, miss. Tuned in to the news straight off which to my mind's more likely to make you miserable than perk you up. But in his case it worked a treat. Right after that he put the doctor's hat on straight, started acting sensible and said it was all a mistake. We see it all here, believe me. That young lady, his solicitor, had no trouble getting him out, pushed him through the back door like last week's washing," he said giving Sylvie a wave as she drove away with her tiresome so-called next-of-kin.

The cottage seemed damp and uncared for, Morrison staring round the room with distaste. Sylvie made a pot of tea but he refused anything to eat, the man's avid gaze taking in Adele's pretty things as if he was seeing everything for the first time.

As they sipped their tea, he visibly relaxed, you could almost say deflated before one's eyes, she reflected.

"What made you suddenly admit you'd lied about killing Ferguson?" she ventured.

His face broke into a smile. "It was on the radio. Toomey had thrown himself into the sea. Some poor bugger trying to save him got dragged off the cliff for his pains and landed at the bottom with him. I knew it would work," he crowed.

Sylvie stiffened. "What would work?"

"Toomey's dead."

"I know that. But he didn't kill himself, Larry. You misunderstood. It was an accident, the railing was rotten. It broke and he and a friend of mine plummeted down the cliff."

"Rubbish. Toomey couldn't stand letting me claim the honour. I knew it would break him."

"What honour?"

"The honour of ending the life of one who never deserved death more."

"Ferguson? You claim to have killed Ferguson just to spite Toomey?" she said, barely containing a shriek of laughter.

"I was lucky my confession made such a splash in the Sunday papers. I didn't do it, of course I didn't. I wanted to kill Ferguson but I'm a coward you see. All talk. Most of us university people are. Toomey was different. I kept track of him after he left prison, watched him get acquainted with Ferguson – he would have to be a saint to forgive that man. He planned to kill him and he carried it out cold-heartedly and with utter venom. I was the only one to suspect him, you know. At first I could only silently applaud and the rest of you were bamboozled including that police inspector woman. They were getting nowhere. But my natural sense of justice won in the end and I worked out a plan. I knew that if *I* claimed to be the murderer Toomey would react in a stupid way, his pride would annihilate his good sense. It worked. He killed himself."

Sylvie dismissed all this as the boasting of a man

unhinged after years of jealousy caused by Adele, a girl she now realised she hadn't really known at all. The motives of all these crazy people were too abstruse for any normal person to understand. She dismissed Morrison's self-congratulation with an impatient shrug and changed the subject, irritated beyond endurance by the man's smug interpretation of his own bizarre input into the Ferguson investigation, not to mention his perception of the alleged suicide of poor Erica's father.

"Will you stay on in Cambridge, Larry? Finish your research?" she asked, stacking the teacups on to the tray, her mind already running ahead to the night's performance.

"I shall live in France. Enjoy my retirement in Adele's farmhouse. I deserve some peace at last. I have already accepted an offer on this cottage. I should have left Cambridge years ago but Adele kept me here, do you see. The few occasions when I might glimpse her in the city made it all worthwhile. But now she's gone."

Sylvie shrugged into her coat, checking her watch as she bent to touch his arm.

"Will you be OK, Larry? I have to go now. Would you like me to ask your neighbour to bring you some eggs or bread or something? You've not eaten properly for days I'm sure."

"I am used to being alone," he said with finality. "It will be easier now I don't have my wife to worry about." As an afterthought he added, "Thank you, Sylvie. May we both enjoy more good fortune now Adele is no longer with us," which, on reflection, seemed an odd benediction.

She drove back to London with her foot firmly on the accelerator, glad to put some mileage between herself and the cast of this extraordinary drama in which Adele had pitched her. The evening performance went well and when the curtain came down it was clear that Garnett's new presentation of that dreary character Hedda Gabler would attract good reviews and a full auditorium. Sylvie was happy to share the success, glad to be a part of the company, overjoyed to find Ian waiting for her clutching a bunch of yellow roses to his chest like an old-fashioned stage door johnnie.

"I've booked a room at the Pheasantry," he whispered. "Game for a sleepless night, my darling?"

She grinned, burying her face in the flowers. "Oh yes. Yes please. I can think of nothing nicer."

They set off to get the car, skirting the park, the air sharp as broken glass. The weather had taken a sudden dive, the temperature plummeting. Sylvie told him about her final meeting with Larry Morrison, her mood serene.

"You seem to have made your peace with Adele too," he ventured, holding her close, their cold breath hanging in the air like cigarette smoke. She shifted her gaze, peering through the railings at the blackness of the empty vista beyond, their pace unhurried.

"Now that it's over I can love her again, Ian. Adele lost me for a while, you know. I felt I had been left out. Cheated somehow. Fancy never telling me about that business of the child's murder in France! Was Adele so shallow that it wasn't important enough to share that with me? I was young then, of course, and would have been less accepting at that age but even so, why not later? Toomey clearly thought she had erased the death from her mind entirely, could barely recall his daughter's name, in fact. I can only take a kinder view. I hope she just couldn't face being diminished in her little sister's eyes and editing out all the gritty bits of her life became a habit I still find difficult accept. Why skate over such a terrible thing as if the child was just a painful incident best forgotten? I was her sister for heaven's sake, existing from hand to mouth in the grittiest business of all, scraping a living with people who do terrible things to each other – I hadn't been living in a convent all those years. Oh, yes, I had my moments when I despaired of knowing what she was really like."

"Time to let it go, Sylvie."

"Morrison wanted me to see my sister as a whole person and he was right. He adored her *despite* everything, saw her as she really was, a girl with murky sides to her personality just like the rest of us. Would I? Adele and I were apart for years, often keeping in touch only by letters and phone calls. We all do it: hide the nasty bits from those we love. Adele probably still regarded me as the kid sister, unsullied by the rough and tumble of real life. You're right, Ian. I do feel at peace with Adele. She suffered after our father died, had to make her way alone. The hard time Adele had to face made her strong but loneliness brought out a side of her I never suspected: ruthless ambition, a touch of greed and a flair for using people if we're being brutally honest. But I loved her. And I love her still. Forgiving is what love's all about, isn't it? None of us is perfect, me least of all."

He squeezed her hand, their steps ringing on the pavement. Sylvie felt energised by this breath of autumn, not the fall she was used to in Canada but the merest hint of the first frost made her blood race.

Ian nodded, brushing her cheek with a kiss, mulling over his own subtle acceptance of love without blame. She was right. Forgiving was the means to start again. Even Morrison had survived to begin a life for himself at last. Sylvie's serenity enfolded them both, his own wretched bitterness since Samantha had gone had somehow dissolved in this new happiness.

He had come home.

Thirty

A year later Kevin Last had still to recover any recollection of that fatal evening which had ended
in Toomey's death. A verdict of accidental death was
brought in without a quibble and an English writer-director
inspired by the Toomey family's tragedy had constructed
a film script still in the throes of competitive bidding
in Tinseltown where it was tipped for the top: Sadie
Marshall-Kent already begging to play Adele.

The darker side of the mystery which would really have
pitched the story into a box-office triumph was never
complete, Kevin's testimony locked up in amnesia. This
was a matter which Sylvie found grimly ironic and a
fair assessment of the film industry's acceptance of the
key witness's alleged blanks. Would Kevin's memory
heal? Sylvie, congenitally sceptical, doubted it, his part
in the film scenario currently sidelined to that of the
cross-dressing partner in a failing restaurant business in
which he was attempting to interest a new backer, the only
reason for his appointment with Toomey at his house by
the sea.

Morrison had wisely gone to ground in Provence, escap-
ing prying eyes with strict security and a reputation as an
unforgiving employer as far as the maintenance of his
privacy was concerned.

Sylvie decided to put down roots at last, absorbing
herself in the challenging Shakespearean roles now open
to her as a member of the Royal Company at Stratford.

215

Kenzo, Ian's ginger cat, moved in with her, deciding that
her house by the river promised more home comforts than
his solitary pursuit of rats in Ian's outbuildings in Suffolk.
Kenzo had quickly tired of the weekly commuting which
this confusing love affair demanded and after going AWOL
on two consecutive Sunday nights when the homegoing cat
basket appeared, Ian decided to let the moggy pick his own
hunting ground and stay put in Shakespeare country. Kenzo
got very fat, in stark contrast to Ian who was far from happy
with this frustrating relationship. He decided he'd apply for
another transfer just as soon as his promotion came through
and Sylvie trusted herself to throw in her lot on a permanent
basis with a man whose career was as unpredictable as her
own. Ian knew at last that meeting Sylvie had saved him
from a downward spiral of bitterness and rancour. His
pride had been given what he thought at the time to be
an emotional death blow but that was all in the past. He
could even joke with his sergeant about improving the locks
on the cottage if only to keep his sock drawer safe from his
ex-wife.

He and Sylvie often visited Le Pendu, delighting in
Kevin's new "family" comprising Ray Colthorpe and
Terry. The place had flourished, the name unchanged, the
prospect of the Toomey film promising publicity which
would thrust the bijou eatery into the limelight and probably
add its name to every tourist's list of "must sees".

"Do you think Kevin has really lost his memory of that
night at Toomey's, Ian? Morrison's theory about Toomey's
involvement has never been aired, has it, but then after
his potty confession anything he had to say would carry
little weight, wouldn't it? The film people badger Kevin
night and day but get short shrift from Larry who only
wishes for a quiet life and will have no truck with the
researchers. I tried to call him myself in the summer
but he wouldn't even speak to me – assured me on
the phone that he was perfectly content with his books

and his writing and relies on his staff to keep every-one out."

"Morrison was lucky to escape so lightly and even Kevin's got away with a limp and a mended skull – he must have sprouted wings to survive that fall. Can't you forget all that, Sylvie? Kevin insists on only living for the future – you can't put your life on perpetual Rewind."

P